THE LIBRARY MYSTERIES

Samuel Holmes has just been promoted to lieutenant of detectives when he and his partner Dr. Watson are assigned a high-profile case — the suspected murder of the deputy mayor's son, whose body has been discovered in the library of an exclusive Victorian-era club. But books are also missing, and it's not long before more historical volumes mysteriously disappear from the city's other libraries. As Sam's team search for clues, they unearth disturbing events from thirty years ago that lead them to uncover a web of torture and murder . . .

Books by Steven Fox
in the Linford Mystery Library:

LEGACIES
THE MISSING NEWLYWEDS
DATA HUNTER
LONELY BUSINESS

STEVEN FOX

THE LIBRARY MYSTERIES

Complete and Unabridged

LINFORD
Leicester

First published in Great Britain

First Linford Edition
published 2019

*A catalogue record for this book is available
from the British Library.*

ISBN 978–1–4448–4267–8

Published by
F. A. Thorpe (Publishing)
Anstey, Leicestershire

Set by Words & Graphics Ltd.
Anstey, Leicestershire
Printed and bound in Great Britain by
T. J. International Ltd., Padstow, Cornwall

This book is printed on acid-free paper

1

The average-looking, middle-aged man told his companion that he was going to try on a couple of blue denim suits in the dressing room at the back of the mall's men's clothing store. He was given permission from the man assigned to watch him. As soon as the man had taken his proposed purchases out of sight of the certified psychological attendant, he used the crowd to slip away and was soon headed past the Museum of Natural and Cultural History and toward the long distance bus terminal.

'I would like to buy a ticket on the next bus to the nearest stop to London, California,' he told the ticket seller. When he was told the amount and had paid the price, he was given his boarding pass and got on the indicated bus. From there he seemed to drop out of sight.

★ ★ ★

Johanna's had a festive atmosphere this night. Johanna herself was presiding. The guest of honor, a young detective and his partner, were in their usual booth.

'How does it feel to be in the supervisors' ranks, Sam?' the young medical examiner sitting beside him asked.

'It's too soon to tell, Jamie,' he replied with a self-deprecating grin. 'Ask me again when I've had the responsibility of a group of detectives on a case.'

Johanna spoke up from her seat across from the two detectives, 'You'll do fine, Sam. Give the team their assignments and let them put the case together while you ask the proper questions. Even Sherlock Holmes had agents to gather the information he needed.'

'And Dr. Watson often made an observation, or asked a question that led him to the proper solution,' Jamie offered, 'even if his conclusions were wrong.'

'Trust your training and your instincts,' Lt. Baker added, 'and you'll do fine.'

The lieutenant's cell phone suddenly demanded attention. He listened a

moment, spoke a few words in reply, and closed the connection.

'Well, Lt. Holmes,' he said as he got up from the table, 'you have your first assignment. You're to take the lead on an apparent homicide at the Victorian Reading Room. The deputy mayor's son has been found dead in the club's library. Your expertise will be useful, too, Dr. Watson.'

The party broke up as Sam and Jamie left the grill and bar and headed for the Victorian-era club on Tenth and Queen Anne Avenues.

'The word is that twenty minutes ago, Jonathan Smythe-Jones, the deputy mayor's son, went into the club's library,' Jamie read the texted information on her phone. 'A few moments later, there was a loud crash. When one of the attendants investigated, he found Smythe-Jones lying on the floor, bleeding from the forehead and the temple.'

'Was the victim still alive when the attendant found him?' Sam questioned.

'The information I have here,' Jamie quickly scrolled through the message, 'doesn't say. We'll have to ask at the scene.'

Sam and Jamie drove the rest of the way in silence.

According to the plaque on the wall, the club's building had been built in 1902. The stucco-covered brick building spanned most of the block on all four sides and had a bar, public, as well as private dining rooms, and a large, well-stocked library.

Sam and Jamie parked as close to the front doors as the other official vehicles would allow. They approached the yellow crime-scene tape and were met by a uniformed officer.

'Lt. Holmes and Dr. Watson,' Sam said as he and Jamie showed their badges and identification. 'Who's working the scene?'

'Detective Sergeant Simon and her partner, Detective Roberts,' the officer replied as he held up the tape to let them pass.

'Julie Simon is a good investigator,' Sam commented as they walked to the library. 'She'll be up for the lieutenant's exam soon. I would like to keep her on the team. And her partner.'

The floor of the library was marked off with grids of string forming one foot squares. The body lay in the center of the grid in a pool of blood.

'Sergeant Simon?' Sam approached the red-headed detective who was interviewing a liveried attendant. The woman held up a hand to signal that she would be with him in a moment. When she finished her interview, she turned to Sam.

'Yes?' She eyed Sam and Jamie as they came closer. 'What can I do for you?'

'I'm Lt. Samuel Holmes and this is my partner, Dr. Jamesina Watson from the FME division. I've been assigned to take the lead in the investigation.'

'That's just great,' she glared at them. 'Jack and I are the first detectives on the scene and you hotshots just come in and take over!'

'I'm not replacing you, Sergeant,' Sam said calmly. 'I would like for you and Detective Roberts to continue the investigation. You'll be part of a larger team whose information will be coordinated by me. Now, can we work together, or would you prefer another assignment?'

'Why would you want to share the glory?'

'Sam isn't about ego,' Jamie spoke up, struggling to stay calm, 'he'd rather see the case solved than allow a criminal a free pass because of a turf war. His ancestor, a famous consulting detective, often allowed others to get the credit for his solves.'

'Besides,' Sam added, 'we're on the same side. What have you got so far?'

Letting out a calming breath, Julie Simon said, 'The victim went into the library to find a book to read. There was a loud noise, as if something heavy had been violently knocked down. When the attendant, a Mr. Rosser, came into the room to check on the noise, he found the victim, Mr. Jonathan Smythe-Jones, lying on the floor bleeding from at least one head wound. A table had apparently been overturned by his fall. It is still uncertain if the victim tripped and hit his head on the table as he fell, or if he was struck down and the table was overturned during a brief struggle.'

'If I may examine the body,' Jamie offered, 'perhaps a preliminary determination can be made.'

Jamie knelt by the dead man. She took a pair of surgical gloves from a pocket and, donning them, began to minutely examine him.

'There are two definite wounds,' she told them. 'The wound on the forehead was possibly caused by striking the table. The temple wound appears to have been delivered from behind by a blunt instrument of some kind. I'll know more after the autopsy.'

'Was the victim alone when the attendant found him?' Sam asked. 'And was he still alive?'

'According to his statement,' Julie said, referring to her notes, 'the victim seemed to expire as he knelt beside him. He doesn't recall seeing anyone in the room. His statement also says that he left the room for a just a moment or so to find a staff member to call 911. He returned to the library and closed it off until the first response teams arrived.'

'So,' Jamie asked, 'it was possible that

someone could have been in hiding and sneaked out before the room was sealed?'

'I would say that it is a very probable scenario,' Sgt. Simon responded. 'A minute would have been ample time for a perp, or a reluctant witness, to have vanished into the crowd.'

Detective Roberts approached the group. 'I've just interviewed all of the staff on duty and most of the members in close proximity to the library. Of those, only two members and three of the staff were aware of anything out of the ordinary until the paramedics and the uniforms arrived.'

'How long between the emergency call and their arrival?' Sam wanted to know.

'Jack,' Sgt. Simon said, 'this is Lt. Samuel Holmes. He will be our lead on this case. And this is his partner, Dr. Jamesina Watson from the FME division.'

'Detective Jack Roberts,' was his even response. 'The patrol officers were five minutes away and began securing the room as soon as they arrived. The EMT's arrived two minutes later. The call interrupted their meal break nearby, hence the quick response times.'

'How soon were the exits secured?' Julie asked her partner. 'Did anyone leave before the uniforms arrived?'

'The manager says that the doors were locked within a minute or two after the time that the attendant gave the alarm,' Detective Roberts replied. 'The doors had to be unlocked to allow the officers and the paramedics inside. No one was seen or reported leaving before then.'

'As soon as everyone has given his or her statement and contact information, you can allow them to leave. Someone will contact them if there is a need for a future interview.'

Sam and Jamie took another look at the body and the crime scene.

'Could both blows have been delivered by the attacker, or even caused by a fall?' Sam asked of Jamie.

'Possibly,' she answered, after taking another look at the scene, 'both blows could have been from an attacker, but not likely from just the fall. I don't think that the attacker caused both head wounds. The overturned table, position of the body, and the gash on the forehead all lead me to believe that Smythe-Jones was struck from behind and struck his head on the table as he fell.'

'We need to find out if anyone heard any verbal altercation before the noise of Mr. Smythe-Jones' fall.'

'None of the patrons or the attendants remembers loud voices,' Sgt. Simon said, walking up to Sam and Jamie. 'I overheard your question just now as I approached to report that the forensics team has arrived.'

'Thank you,' Jamie said as she turned to Sam. 'I'll stay and confer with the team and their doctor. I'd like to see if he, or she, independently agrees with my findings. The SID may find some things of interest.'

'I'll notify the family,' Sam volunteered before he looked at Julie. 'Unless you want to do it, Sergeant?'

'I would like to go along, Lieutenant,' Julie responded. 'I've known the family for a long time. Jonathan's sister and I went to school together and shared several of the same teachers.'

'It might help the family to see a familiar face at a time like this,' Sam agreed. 'Let's allow everyone to do their jobs here while we visit the family. We don't want them to learn about something like this from the media hounds.'

★ ★ ★

The Smythe-Jones family were all at home when Sam and Julie arrived at their well-kept, split-level home. Sam noticed that Julie was more nervous than he thought she should have been as he rang the doorbell, which was answered by a uniformed housekeeper.

'Miss Julie,' she said smilingly as she saw who was at the door. 'Who is your friend?'

'This is Lt. Samuel Holmes, Samantha,' Julie's voice quivered slightly as she spoke. 'Is the family all here? We've come on official business with unpleasant news.'

Samantha's expression changed as she opened the door completely and stood aside to let them in.

'I'll ask everyone to meet you in the Master's study,' she said without any seeming emotion as she left them to gather the family members.

'At least we only have to make one notification,' Julie sniffed. 'I've never had to notify a family of the death of a loved one that I knew personally before.'

'They're never easy,' Sam allowed. 'A homicide notification is the hardest, along with the accidental death of a young child.'

The Smythe-Jones family entered and the deputy mayor spoke. 'Julie, Samantha says you have some unpleasant news to tell us.'

Julie lost her composure and began to weep. 'Sir, I'm very sorry, but your son Jonathan was killed in the library of the Victorian Reading Room not more than an hour ago.'

Mrs. Smythe-Jones, face contorted in agony and disbelief, collapsed into a nearby chair. Samantha began sobbing uncontrollably.

'Was it an accident?' Jonathan's sister, Bobbie, asked.

'Our investigation has just begun,' answered Sam with professional calmness, 'but we don't think so. It appears that he may have been murdered.'

'But why Jonathan?' The deputy mayor's face was ashen. 'He was never involved with violent people and there have been no threats recently that I'm aware of.'

'Yes, sir, the department is aware of the crank letters and calls of five years ago,' Julie said.

'At this time,' Sam added, 'we believe that your son was the unfortunate victim of being in the wrong place at the wrong time. The forensics team is going over the library room now. Dr. Watson and her team will check all of the evidence when the autopsy is finished.'

'You're certain that it was Jonathan?' Bobbie tearfully inquired. 'He was so ecstatic when he was accepted as a member of the club. He loved old books and he knew that members had exclusive access to the rare first and second editions of the published journals of the city's founding fathers.'

'We'll be doing an inventory of the

library's books and journals,' Sam replied. 'Julie was one of the first investigators on the scene.'

'Julie?'

'Yes,' Julie said. 'It was definitely your brother. He and I were too close when we were dating in high school for me not to know him on sight.'

'Oh, Miss Julie,' Samantha sobbed into her uniform's apron, 'this must be as hard for you, as it is for the family and me!'

Julie could no longer keep her composure and found a seat and wept inconsolably.

'Even though we went our separate ways after high school, we remained close friends,' she said through her tears. 'I came here, intending to be strong and consoling. And look at me.'

'It's never easy having to relay this kind of news, Julie.' Smythe-Jones put a hand on Julie's shoulder. 'Thank you for being willing to be here at this time.'

'Sir,' Sam interrupted, 'perhaps our questions can wait a day or two so you can begin to come to grips with your grief and also give us time, hopefully, to have a few answers for you.'

Julie was exceptionally quiet on the way back to the Victorian Reading Room. Sam left her to her thoughts.

She probably shouldn't have been a part of the notification team, he mused. If he had known how close she was to the deceased and his family, he'd have asked her partner to come with him, instead.

★   ★   ★

When Sam and Julie had arrived back at the Victorian Reading Room, Detective Roberts and the uniforms were just finishing up their questioning of all potential witnesses and the forensics team was almost finished examining the scene.

'Do we know if anything is missing?' Julie asked. 'We understand that there were some valuable volumes among the collection.'

'Nothing certain, yet,' Jack replied. 'But there are possibly a few volumes that haven't been accounted for yet. The library records are being reviewed to be sure that nothing was loaned out that was supposed to have remained on site.'

'What are the volumes that haven't been accounted for?' questioned Sam.

'A set of histories on the early settlement of immigrants after a conglomerate of disillusioned British subjects bought the land on which London, California was settled.'

'When were these histories published?' Julie asked.

'The three-volume, first edition was published in 1903 by a now defunct British publishing company,' Jack told her.

'So these three volumes are worth money?' Jamie asked as she joined the group.

'Possibly a quarter of a million for the set,' Jack revealed, 'and historically invaluable to the city.'

'Something that would be hard to fence?' Jamie asked for further information.

'The buyer could never place them on display,' Sam offered. 'It would have to be someone who would just want to possess them or to ask a heavy ransom.'

'Too bad our most intriguing snitch is

away at the Pulitzer Prize Awards convention,' Jamie commented. 'Who would have thought that sleazy tabloid muckraker had it in him?'

'He proved himself to be a top-notch investigative reporter after all,' agreed Sam.

'You mean that reporter from the *Midnight Confessor*?' Jack questioned. 'I heard that his editor fired him and is looking to hire a replacement.'

'The editor may be looking for a replacement,' Sam replied, 'but not because he fired the sleazy, dirty old man. He's afraid that some big city paper will offer him big bucks to come to work for them.'

'Well,' Julie said, 'good riddance to bad trash. He made my skin crawl whenever I got near him.'

'I feel the same way,' Jamie added, 'but he came through for me and Sam during the Super-TASER and Missing Newlyweds cases. He was almost killed twice.'

'Maybe so,' Julie offered, 'but I feel unclean around him, somehow.'

'A snitch's usefulness has little to do

with his, or her, likeability,' Sam added his opinion. 'What matters is how reliable the information is.'

'Now we just need to find a reliable source on fences of hard to sell goods,' Jack sighed.

'Everyone get some rest,' Sam ordered. 'Tomorrow morning we'll meet in Conference Room 'B' and go over our notes and the forensics report. When can we have a preliminary report, Jamie?'

'I think we can have the initial study done by morning if we push for priority. The toxicology and DNA labs are running a backlog of about two weeks. I don't think we can get those reports for at least that long.'

'Okay.' Sam made some notes. 'We'll meet at 10 o'clock and begin brainstorming. Anything else? No? Then I'll see everyone in the morning.'

With a look, Sam asked Jamie to stay behind. After the others had left, Sam voiced his concerns about Julie's involvement with the Smythe-Joneses.

'Julie has known the deceased's family for a good deal of her life and, I gather, had an intense relationship with Jonathan during high school. They may have been closer than either of them realized. Julie broke down while we were there. Perhaps you and she should find time for a heart-to-heart chat.'

'You're concerned that her emotions may affect her focus?' Jamie considered her observations of the woman. 'From what I've seen, her professionalism should keep her on track. Her earlier hostility may have been because she knew the victim so intimately. When the investigation still appeared to be in her hands, it seemed to abate. I'll discreetly find out how close she was to Jonathan and what their current relationship was.'

'And just maybe, she's too close to the situation. If she is, I'd prefer to find out sooner rather than later. She has too good a record to allow a black mark on her career now.'

'I'll do what I can, Sam.'

2

That night, Sam booted up his recently purchased laptop computer and logged on to the department's information network services. Jamie had spent several hours helping him to download what he needed to have at his fingertips and instructing him in how to use the files and programs efficiently.

While he had above-average computer skills, his information search and retrieval skills, even now, needed improvement. He decided to first find out what he could about Jonathan Smythe-Jones' background and personal history.

'No large Facebook friends list,' he murmured to himself as he worked. 'But a lot of activity with those on his list. Cautiously gregarious. His personal information is under high security parameters, and he appears to be reasonably computer savvy. No other social network accounts found. Perhaps Wikipedia has a page on him.'

While Jonathan was a highly visible personality locally, no one seemed to rate him important enough to need information from that source.

'Let's see what a Google search comes up with,' he mumbled as he typed in his search parameters.

After winnowing down all of the hits provided, Sam finally found what he was looking for.

Valedictorian for his high school graduating class, accepted into Boston University's law school, he read. Specialized in city government. Graduated with honors. Worked on the city council's legal renovation project for two years. Also ran for a council seat but lost by a narrow margin.

Seemed like a civic minded person. Too busy for Julie perhaps? Maybe he'd have a private talk to Jack while Jamie had her chat with Julie.

After using various search engines for two hours without finding much more than a standard biography, Sam closed down his computer and went to bed.

Having arrived early the next morning,

Sam set up a whiteboard, a corkboard, and had an urn of coffee and a pot of hot water with several bags of regular and herbal tea brought in. To this, he added a large box of doughnuts and other pastries.

While he waited for the others to arrive, he went over the facts that had been gathered from the day before. On the whiteboard, he prepared a flowchart of events, a list of the victim's known associates and family, and his recent activities. He was certain that the rest of his team would have information to add when they arrived.

A few minutes before ten, Jamie, Julie and Jack came into the conference room and chose a beverage and a pastry. After viewing the two boards, they found seats around the table.

'That's fairly informative for overnight info-gathering,' Jack commented after looking over the case boards. 'You get most of the bio from the internet?'

'I also told him that Jonathan and I were very close during high school,' Julie replied. 'What I didn't tell him, and haven't revealed until now, is that we had what used to be called 'an understanding' before he went back East to the university.

'While we remained close friends,' she continued, 'we had drifted apart by the time he finished at Boston University and returned home. Things had changed between us and our goals had gone in different directions. He went into city government and I into went into law enforcement. And, yes, I believe that I can be objective.'

'I'll accept that for now,' Sam stated. 'I'll expect to be informed if anything changes.'

The meeting got underway with Julie providing deep background on Jonathan's past while both Julie and Jack updated the information on his family and circle of friends.

'After Jonathan lost his bid for a council seat,' Jack said, 'he became an advocate for legal reform. He believed that our civil and criminal codes needed updating to reflect changes in technology and ethical standards.'

'He also pushed for stricter controls on the newly decriminalized medical usage of cannabis and its manufacture,' Julie added. 'His ideas were met with mixed results.'

'Could someone have used the theft of the books as a cover-up for a vendetta?' Sam asked.

'Possibly,' Julie answered, 'but not likely. As far as anyone knows, he had no enemies, politically or personally, even though his views were considered controversial by some.'

'I checked with the Reading Room on the missing books,' Jamie added. 'They were valuable, but mainly as historical collectors' items. A legal market would have been small and very selective. If an unscrupulous buyer could be found, the death of Smythe-Jones would very likely have warned him, or her, off of the sale because of possibly being an accessory after the fact.'

'Let's move on to the preliminary autopsy and forensics reports,' Sam said, wanting to keep the meeting progressing. 'Jamie?'

'The cause of death was due to severe intracranial trauma,' she reported, 'caused by a severe blow to the right temple from behind, followed by a second blow to the frontal lobe, most likely caused by striking the corner of the table as the victim fell. Either blow could have caused a debilitating trauma and possibly death. The two together made death an almost certainty.'

'Murder may not have been intended?' Jack queried.

'Hard to prove intent,' Jamie replied.

'When we find this person, we'll go with a charge of first degree murder,' Sam added. 'A death caused in the commission of a crime has long been upheld as a felony by the courts.'

'The only hard DNA evidence at the scene,' Julie offered 'was from the victim. There was no struggle evident, and too many fingerprints from too many people to be helpful. Our perp could have been one of a thousand people who used the library.'

'Access to standard fictional items was given to anyone with a public Reading

Room library card,' Jack informed the group. 'However, certain volumes were not allowed out of the library and available only to members of the club with special privileges listed on their cards during library hours. They were not checked out. The missing volumes were definitely stolen.'

'No chance of them having been sent out for repairs or such?'

'None, according to the library's archivist.'

The crime flowchart and list of known associates was updated and the discussion changed to speculation of events and relationships between family members.

'I know that SOP says 'look at the family members first',' Julie said, 'but having known them most of my life, I have a hard time believing that one of them could have done such a horrible thing.'

'No violent anger,' Sam prompted, 'or smoldering animosity evident in the family dynamic?'

'None that I recognized beyond the normal back and forth of any group of people placed in daily close proximity,' she answered. 'Jonathan was the most even tempered of them all to my knowledge. I can't recall any voices raised in anger, even when there were strong disagreements.'

'What was the nature of the disagreements?' Jamie wanted to know.

'Until Jonathan returned from the East Coast, it was the usual. How late he stayed out, his choice of friends. That sort of thing.'

'How about after his return from university?' Sam inquired. 'Any strong feelings expressed then?'

'Some on political issues,' Julie admitted, 'but they usually agreed to disagree agreeably.'

'Who was the most vocal in disagreeing with him?'

'I believe his sister was,' Julie said after a moment of reflection. 'And even then, they were more in the nature of highly spirited debate.'

'What about close friends or political rivals?' Jack asked. 'Any hard feelings there?'

'Nothing that seemed to go beyond normal politics,' was Julie's response. 'Most of the animosities seemed to dissipate after the elections.'

'So,' Sam said, 'we're back to Smythe-Jones being in the wrong place at the wrong time?'

'It would appear so,' the others agreed.

3

The London City University library was dark, quiet and supposedly unoccupied on a late weekend-night. The campus police officer checked the doors during a routine patrol. From out of a dark alcove, a lone figure came up behind the officer and, using a no longer authorized police chokehold for controlling violent suspects, rendered him unconscious.

Using the key to the door that the attacker had appropriated earlier, the lone figure entered the rare book section. After a quick perusal of the shelves, he selected two books and quickly left the way he had come, relocking the doors he had opened.

Shortly after the thief had made his escape, the officer came to his senses. Using his two-way radio, he notified his superiors of the attack and his location. The Robbery-Homicide division of the city police was also notified.

By the time Sam and his team arrived,

the library had been inspected by the rare book archivist and the two volumes were discovered missing.

'What were the books about?' the library's rare book archivist was asked.

'From the position on the shelf,' he said, 'the records of the local water table compiled over the last century or so.'

'How valuable were these books?' Jack inquired.

'Not much monetarily,' the librarian responded, 'but the importance, economically, of predicting the underground water levels in response to the city's growth in population is paramount.'

The university police officer could not add anything beyond the report that he had made to his superiors upon regaining consciousness.

'All that I know,' he related upon being questioned, 'is that I was about to check the library doors when I felt pressure around my throat and everything went black.'

'You heard nothing?' Julie asked. 'No footsteps or heavy breathing? Nothing that caught your eye that made you decide to check the doors?'

'It was a routine check during my rounds,' the officer answered. 'I think that I caught a strong whiff of aftershave. Possibly something like 'Brute'.'

'What sort of thief would use aftershave just before pulling a late-night heist?' Julie wondered aloud.

'Maybe he had an assignation near that time?' was Jamie's response.

'A man with lots of chutzpa,' Sam said, 'that's for certain. Why set up an important meeting with someone just before, or just after, he committed his theft?'

After the forensics team finished with the crime scene, Sam told everyone to write up their reports and to meet again the next afternoon in the conference room.

The next morning, Sam had a meeting with Lt. Baker in his office.

'The investigations are still young,' he told the older man, 'but none of the evidence feels right. It makes no sense.'

'How so?' Baker asked.

'The books that have been taken,' Sam

replied, 'while important to the city in some way, and out of print, are not extremely valuable or overtly rare. And yet, murder was apparently committed during the first set of thefts. Also, the types of volumes taken are not what a collector would normally be willing to steal to get, nor would they be easy to fence.'

After the team had gotten their lunches, everyone met in the same conference room as the day before.

'Our perp is bold,' Julie said disgustedly. 'He's hit two of the city's libraries in less than forty-eight hours. The first was while it was still daylight, and the second in the dead of night when everything was locked up.'

'Are there any members of the club who would also have access to the university library after hours?' Julie asked. 'There was no evidence of forced entry. The patrol officer was only incapacitated temporarily by that chokehold.'

'That's another thing to check,' Sam told his team, 'do any of the people with access to both libraries have police or military training that would include knowing how to use that particular method of subduing someone? Jamie, I want you and Julie to check our persons of interest backgrounds. Jack, you and I will canvass the areas and see if any new information turns up.'

Julie and Jamie decided to use Julie's departmentally issued unmarked vehicle to return to the Reading Room. During the drive, they talked about what they knew so far. Before they arrived, they had begun to talk about, and to ask questions about, their partners.

'Jack has a chivalrous side that can be sweet,' Julie told Jamie, 'but it can also be very exasperating. When we were first partnered together, he needed to be the big, macho protector of his 'weaker' female partner. In spite of my greater experience.'

'It looks like the two of you have worked that out,' Jamie took the opportunity to learn more. 'How long have you worked together?'

'It's been three years now,' was Julie's response. 'We eventually learned to see each other as equals, but with different strengths. How long have known Sam?'

'Captain Reynolds put us together about a year ago,' Jamie replied. 'He realized that he had a Holmes and a Watson in the department and thought that it would be advantageous to team us together on the Super-TASER case. During that case, we realized that we were both direct descendants of the original Sherlock Holmes and Dr. Watson.'

'That must have been interesting.'

'It certainly turned out that way,' Jamie elaborated. 'As it happened, an old enemy from Sam's high school days was the leader of the group that had stolen the Super-TASER and knew that the original Holmes and Watson were not fictional characters. He decided to eliminate the last of the Holmes family and all three living generations of the Watson family, which included my then three-year-old nephew.'

'I can see that he failed,' Julie said.

'But he came close to taking Sam's life and I was also badly wounded. During the final confrontation, Sam and his nemesis both suffered deadly knife wounds. The other man died at the scene and Sam came close to bleeding to death.'

'It sounds as if the two of you bonded pretty well,' Julie observed.

'We did,' Jamie agreed. 'But the real bond was between my nephew, Jimmy, and Sam. Jimmy had to be literally kept away from the hospital so the doctors could do their jobs in helping Sam to get well. Sam convinced his doctors, once he was out of danger, that visits from his young friend would be advantageous to both of them.'

Julie and Jamie arrived at the Victorian Reading Room, parked the car, and went inside. The crime scene tape had been removed, but the crowd remained smaller than usual.

As they walked to the concierge station, whispered conversations about what had transpired in the library were overheard.

'I heard that Smythe-Jones surprised a thief and was killed as he left to tell one of the attendants,' one person was heard to say in a hushed voice.

'I heard that he was killed because he and his co-conspirator had a falling out,' said another.

Julie and Jamie made mental notes of the rumors they heard and made a special effort to remember the faces of the ones who were spreading them.

'All of this innuendo and suspicion can't be helping the deputy mayor and his family,' Jamie remarked with a sympathetic sigh.

'I'm not sure that they know about the rumors,' Julie told her. 'They've been cloistered since the family requested to be left alone to grieve until the body is released and funeral arrangements can be made.'

The concierge greeted them politely and, after hearing what Julie and Jamie needed, agreed to give them just the minimum amount of information allowed about the club members.

'We do have confidentiality agreements with our members,' he explained. 'Of course we will comply with any court order, but our 'right of privacy' agreements are part of a binding contract.'

'We are just looking for general information at the moment,' Julie explained. 'Just things like how many of your members have military or law enforcement backgrounds.'

'No names?'

'If we decide that we require names,' Jamie replied, 'we'll get as much as we can from public sources before seeking stronger requests. We also need to speak with the attendants who were on duty at the time of Smythe-Jones' death.'

Because of their duties, it took some time to re-interview the attendants. The one who gave the alarm was a dignified, gray-haired man in his late fifties. When he was asked about any military or law enforcement experience he told them that, due to a shattered kneecap in a bicycle accident in his teens, he had been disqualified for either career.

'My family was more likely to be employed in the domestic or service industries,' he further explained. 'I've been employed by the club for a number of years and I have a good record here.'

'Tell us what happened on the day you

found Mr. Smythe-Jones,' Julie asked.

'I had just finished surveying the room to see if any tables needed bussing or if a member required anything,' the attendant told them. 'The door to the library was slightly ajar. As I approached to check the library, I heard a loud noise and immediately entered.'

'And how did you find the deceased, Mr. Rosser?' Jamie queried.

'At first glance,' Mr. Rosser, the attendant, replied, 'the room seemed unoccupied and perfectly normal. As I was looking more closely around the room, I heard a moan as if someone were in pain. It was then that I saw that one of the reading tables by the far wall to my right had been overturned and that a body lay on the floor beside it. I rushed over to check on the person. When I arrived, poor Mr. Smythe-Jones appeared to have breathed his last.'

'And what did you do then?' Julie prompted.

'I looked for someone to call the emergency number. I found Mr. Nichols, the other roving attendant, and gave him all of the information I could, returned to the library to lock the door, and waited for the professionals to arrive.'

'How long do you think that the library was unsecured before you returned?'

'No more than a minute or two, I think. You always think that your training will keep you calm and in control, but reality has a way of shattering your expectations.'

Jamie and Julie thanked Mr. Rosser and interviewed Attendant Nichols and the manager without learning anything new.

'Perhaps,' Jamie said to Julie, 'we need to find out what the deputy mayor and his family knows about his recent activities and associates.'

'I wish we could put off questioning them.' Julie looked unsure of herself. 'But I don't think this will get any easier by putting it off. I really hate interviewing the victim's family members. Especially a family I practically grew up with.'

★   ★   ★

Sam and Jack talked with the campus police's shift supervisor before meeting the officer who was on duty the night of the break-in. They were given a copy of the officer's activity log and incident report.

'He's actually one of our more experienced people on the third watch,' said the supervisor, a middle-aged man whose wiry, black hair was beginning to turn gray, and whose eyes had wrinkles caused by years of seeing his share of mankind's seamy side. However, he still had a positive and pleasant attitude. 'When he reported having been attacked, I took it seriously. I sent back-up immediately with orders to assist Officer Johnston in securing the scene and to assess his physical condition. He was standing in front of the library doors, which were locked. Officer Johnston reported that he had found them that way when regained his senses. The librarian was awakened and asked to bring his keys so that the library could be opened by the time your people arrived.'

'Was the building checked before the

Robbery-Homicide officers arrived?' Jack inquired as he took notes and Sam watched the Campus Police shift supervisor's body language.

'Yes, sir,' he was told. 'Two of the campus police and I went through the building to clear it before the librarian was allowed in to see if he could ascertain if anything had been taken or vandalized. Between the facts that the locked doors indicated that our perp had already gone, and that there was no sign of vandalism, the only indication of illegal entry was the two empty spaces on the shelves where the books no longer in print were located. There were no scratches around the locks.'

'And our forensics people found no indication of a jimmy or lock-pick having been used,' Sam agreed. 'What about Officer Johnston? Any physical marks on him?'

'The paramedics found a small bruise on his throat and his uniform had stains showing indications of his having been dragged across the grass. He said that when he came to, he was under the hedge

41

that borders the front of the library.'

'What about other keys to the library?' Sam queried. 'How many people have access? Were the shelves the books were stolen from also secured?'

'The Head Librarian would have that information,' he was told, 'but the book shelves were part of a glass case. I don't remember seeing any locking device on it. I do know that our officers don't have keys to any of the buildings. If we have reason to enter a building after hours, it's usually because someone has broken in, and we normally find indications of vandalism along with any missing items.'

Sam and Jack thanked the campus police supervisor and walked over to the library office. After notifying the desk clerk that they wished to speak with the Head Librarian about the break-in and theft, they were shown to an office marked 'Suzanne Waters, Head Librarian'.

They were greeted by a comfortably late-middle-aged woman in a conservative pantsuit and sensible shoes. Her smile was genuine, but stressed, as she asked the two investigators to be seated.

'We won't interfere with your schedule any more than we can help,' Sam said as he and Jack sat down in the visitors' chairs. 'We need to ask a few questions about last night's break-in.'

'Yes,' Ms. Waters said. 'Isn't it sad that a university library isn't safe from people who can't leave other people's property alone?'

'Can you tell me how many people have keys, or might have access to keys for the library? Also, the shelves from which the books were taken — were they secured in any way?'

'Just a sliding lock to secure the glass doors on the case,' Waters told him. 'The division heads and I all have keys and there is a set that checks out to those who are authorized and have need, such as the Dean of Students.'

'How did the university acquire the water table records?' Jack wondered.

'We received several volumes from the estate of one of our former graduates,' Waters replied. 'Many of our books have been gifts.'

'Would you please ask the other people responsible for keys to the library if they have any reason to believe that their keys may have been taken and copied?' Sam asked. 'We would like to eliminate any possibility of an extra set of keys having been made. We also need the check-out and return records of the loaner keys.'

'Surely you don't think that one of our people is responsible?'

'Not necessarily Ms. Waters,' Jack spoke up quickly, 'but an irresponsible person may have taken advantage of a careless moment to obtain a set of his or her own.'

After a few more questions, Sam and Jack left their calling cards along with a request that if Ms. Waters, or any of her staff, thought of anything that could be helpful, to get in touch with one of them.

4

In the out-of-print book section, the slim, nondescript, middle-aged man looked carefully about his surroundings. Seeing that no one was paying attention, he quickly unlocked the case and placed a volume in his backpack. The City Library security system may as well not have existed, he had planned so well. His backpack had a special lining that blocked the electronic sensors that would alarm if a book were to be taken without having proper pre-authorization. Also, the locked case had not been alarmed. A simple lock was all the protection on these semi-valuable books.

No one had seen him take the volume on rainfall records and, walking past the detectors at the door, he went east to Central Boulevard, headed south, and disappeared from view.

At the library's closing time, the locked glass doors of the rare and out-of-print book shelves were checked. The blank space where the missing book of rainfall records had been was noticed. The library clerk checked at the desk for the missing volume. The book was not there, and no one had been reported as requesting it.

'It may have been stolen,' the clerk told her Branch Head. 'Haven't the other libraries in the city reported thefts of out-of-print volumes?'

'Yes, they have,' the librarian remarked. 'I think they all had something to do with old city records. I'll notify the police department immediately.'

Jamie and Julie were headed back to the station when they were told by the dispatcher to see the Branch Head at the City Library.

'It sounds like we may have another missing book,' they were informed.

Since the library was only a block northwest of the police station, the two detectives went there directly.

'Do we put in for overtime?' Julie asked half-humorously. 'It's been a long and emotionally draining three days. At least it has been for me.'

'Talk to Sam when we're done,' Jamie replied with a mischievous grin. 'That's part of his new responsibilities since his promotion. And he just loves paperwork.'

The library clerk and the Branch Head were waiting when Julie and Jamie arrived. They opened the doors when the Branch Head recognized Jamie from her many hours of doing research with Sam.

'In a way,' she remarked as she closed and relocked the doors, 'you and Sergeant Holmes have spent enough time here to know our procedures as well as any of the staff.'

'Sam has been promoted to lieutenant now, Mrs. Brinks,' Jamie informed her pleasantly. 'He's heading the investigations. Sergeant Julie Simmons, her partner, Detective Jack Roberts, and I are all part of his team.'

'That's good to hear. He deserves it.'

'We were told that one of your out-of-print books is missing,' Julie politely interrupted. 'When was the volume discovered missing, and which one was it?'

'It's not one you would think that

someone would want to steal,' the library clerk responded. 'It was just a locally published record of our rainfall from the city's founding until around 1995.'

'I wonder if there might be someone who feels that the water rights may have been manipulated and his or her fortunes have been affected adversely,' Julie pondered. 'This dry lake was originally believed to be totally dried up. Then one of the farmers hired a waterwitch to search for any sign of water.'

'That was in 1895,' Mrs. Brinks recalled. 'The locals got together and dug down a few feet and discovered potable water in enough volume that it was estimated at the time to be able to sustain a regulated, but growing, economy with its attendant population for approximately two hundred years. That was the beginning of London's boomtown era. The First World War brought a lot of light industry and the dry desert air made us a place where a lot of people came for their health. The city council hired engineers and specialists to predict the growing city's needs in the future and to regulate 'growth and water usage.'

'The whole history sounds far-sighted to me,' Jamie said. 'I wouldn't have believed that anyone was thinking much about the water supply as part of the area's limited resources back then.'

'Several of the founding fathers had been soldiers during campaigns in the Sahara and other dry places,' Mrs. Brinks informed them. 'They had learned hard lessons about the importance of a reliable water supply. Many had begun to make ordinances about water conservation.'

'Are there any records of the earliest settlers of the area?' Jamie inquired. 'A list of names or any land grants or deeds?'

'Are you thinking that someone may have felt that they had been taken advantage of because of the way in which the water was discovered?' Julie wondered.

'There once was a record book of land purchases,' Mrs. Brinks said after thinking for several moments, 'but I think that it was sold at an auction to raise money for the new building several years ago.'

'Is there any way to find out who it was

sold to?' Jamie was anxious to know. 'Or if perhaps we could find a second copy?'

'You could check the City Archives,' Mrs. Brinks told the detectives. 'Back then, duplicate records were kept just in case of fire, or other damage, to the court house.'

The city's records archive was in the basement of the City Hall, which was only a couple of blocks southeast of the library. Julie and Jamie would have taken a walk, but they realized that if the library was closed, City Hall would also be closed to the public.

'I guess we can wait until they're open in the morning,' Jamie said. 'It's not like we have a dire emergency on our hands.'

'Perhaps it would be a good idea to catch up on what Jack and Sam have found out,' Julie added. 'Maybe they have found a new piece to our three-way puzzle.'

*   *   *

Sam and Jack pulled into the detectives' parking lot just as Jamie and Julie were getting out of their vehicle. They all acknowledged the presence of the others and headed into the station.

When they reached Sam's office cubicle, he invited them all to find a place to sit down.

'I heard the dispatcher inform you about the City Library call,' he opened the informal meeting. 'Did it turn out to be related to our current investigation?'

'It's a definite possibility,' Jamie replied. 'Mrs. Brinks said that the missing book was an out-of-print record of rainfall in the area for nearly a hundred years.'

'Jamie has surmised that the six volumes may have been taken by a descendant of someone who felt his family was cheated out of his land and water rights,' Julie added.

'It would be a reasonable conclusion,' Jack agreed. 'Human nature wasn't any different in the late nineteenth or early twentieth centuries than it is now.'

'Any hope of finding duplicate records?' Sam questioned.

'City Hall may have kept back-up records on things like land grants and changes of ownership,' Jamie answered, 'just in case of damage to the originals. Mrs. Brinks made the suggestion.'

'Jamie and I,' Julie quickly added, 'were planning a visit to the basement records room of City Hall in the morning. I don't believe records that old have been recorded electronically yet.'

'Good thinking,' Sam replied. 'Jack and I may have some ideas as to how the university library was entered. The perp may have appropriated a set of keys and made a wax impression before returning them. I also believe that all three thefts are related. All six volumes are connected, in one way or another, to information pertaining to the water table or rainfall records here in London.'

'And Jonathan's death?' Julie wanted to know.

'Definitely a homicide in the commission of a felony theft,' Sam said. 'We find the thief, we find his killer. I want you and Jamie to pursue Jonathan's murder. Jack and I will continue to find out what we can about the thefts.'

5

In his rented apartment, the slim, middle-aged and nondescript man sat in his easy chair under the reading lamp. As he read, he made notes and compared them with those he had made from the other books he had stolen.

He had discovered that at least a dozen farmers were bought out or forced off their properties. Not one of them had received a tenth of its eventual worth! They had no idea of the water-wealth under their land.

The man dropped the book and his notes angrily on the floor and agitatedly paced the apartment.

'I'll find some way to make the city make restitution!' he told himself. 'All of those people were cheated. We deserve to be compensated. Now I've almost got enough evidence to pursue legal action. That pompous Jonathan Smythe-Jones got his just deserts when he saw me taking those books at the Club's reading room. He wouldn't just let me gather my evidence in peace. No, he had to threaten to expose me.'

The man continued to convince himself that his ends justified his means.

Finally, the man settled down and decided to find a place to relax and have a nice meal. Johanna's was closer than the Victorian Reading Room or Mom and Pop's Café, so he decided to go there.

★ ★ ★

Sam and Jamie walked into Johanna's just after the evening rush. Out of habit, they both gave the dining area a quick once-over as they went to a booth near the back wall. At the counter, they both spotted a stranger. He obviously was avoiding making eye contact with either of them as they passed by. When his order was placed before him, he studiously concentrated on his meal, neither looking up from his plate nor to either side. When he was finished, he left a large tip on the counter, picked up his check, and went to the cash register. He paid his bill, received his change, and walked out of the door; all without saying a word or looking at anyone.

'Did you notice the man who just left?' Sam asked Jamie.

'You mean the one dressed all in blue denim?' Jamie responded. 'He did act like he didn't wish to be noticed, didn't he?'

'He especially didn't want *us* to make eye contact or engage him in conversation.'

'Do you think he just doesn't like the company of strangers, or was he just avoiding cops?'

The waiter approached their table with their usual beverages and opened up his order book.

'The evening special of ham steaks and potatoes au gratin is the new chef's specialty,' he informed them. 'And the pastry chef has outdone herself tonight on your favorites.'

'We'll each have the special,' Sam said after a quick nod from Jamie, 'and some information, Mike.'

'Go ahead and place their order on the

wheel, Mike,' the tall, dark-haired owner said as she came up and sat down with the two detectives. 'I'm sure that they're hungry after a long day.'

Mike bowed slightly and left to do as she asked.

'Now,' Johanna stated with a cautious look, 'what would you like to know, about whom, and why?'

'The gentleman wearing the blue denim outfit who just left,' Sam told her, 'he looked new in town and didn't seem very sociable.'

'He's been in a few times,' Johanna said. 'Always sits alone at the counter, eats his dinner, and leaves. Big tipper, but as you said, not very sociable. Been coming in for two or three weeks. The only people I've seen him say more than half a dozen words to have been some of the old-timers.'

'Any idea what he talks about with these old-timers?' Sam questioned.

'I couldn't tell you, but Old Man Van Cole sure could!' Johanna answered. 'The stranger talked his ear off for two hours a few nights ago.'

'Have you seen Old Man Van Cole tonight?' Jamie wondered.

Johanna looked at the door as an elderly, fit man in his late seventies or early eighties, and about six feet tall, walked in with a steady gait. 'There he is now. Shall I invite him over?'

'Yes,' was Sam's enthusiastic reply. 'He may have picked up some information relating to a case we're working on.'

'The Smythe-Jones murder?'

'And some possibly related book thefts from all of the libraries.'

Johanna left the table to greet Old Man Van Cole and relay Sam and Jamie's invitation.

The old man shook hands with the two detectives after Johanna made the introductions. The old man's weathered face was friendly and expressive. His eyes were surrounded with lines from both the sun and laughter.

'What can I help you young folks with?' His voice was strong and clear. His speech was that of a mostly self-taught man.

'We're interested in a newcomer to our

fair city,' Sam answered. 'He seems to be interested in the old-timers. Otherwise, he seems unsociable.'

'You must mean 'Blue Man',' Van Cole said. 'Took me more than a week to get him to say more'n a dozen words. Then, about two nights ago, the dam busted. He talked and asked questions for what seemed like half the night. Seemed to know a little about 'most all of the folks that lived here during the days of the water-witch findings. Kept asking about which families made how much off the water rights and who got bought out so that they'd move on.'

'Seems to be a strange set of interests,' Jamie observed. 'Did he seem interested in any other local news, such as library books, or possibly books from private collections having gone missing recently?'

'He did ask about the deputy mayor's son's death. Seemed curious about what was being said around town and what the constabulary was doing about it.'

The discussion continued for several minutes until the detectives orders were brought to the table. Van Cole was invited to join them and reminisce about his boyhood in the city during the war years.

'The government boys couldn't tell the difference between the different Asiatic groups,' Van Cole told them, 'so they just rounded up any Asian they could find, confiscated their land, and put them in the camps. No due process at all. They didn't care how long any of 'em had lived in this country, either. They looked like Tojo, so they were the enemy. The Germans and Eye-talians, as long as they had no accent and looked like 'real Americans', could blend in better and so they had things a little easier.'

'Hate anyone who looks or sounds like the enemy,' Sam commented, 'and don't get confused by the facts. It must have been a terrible time to look or sound different.'

'A lot of kids my age couldn't understand why they couldn't play or talk to certain kids they had lived with in the same neighborhood all of their lives,' Old Man Van Cole informed them. 'They just did what their parents told them and believed that whatever they said was right and true. Grown-ups weren't questioned by children in those days. 'Children are seen, not heard' we were told.'

'What was said by the old folks about London's beginnings and discovery of the water underground?' Jamie asked. 'Were people run off their property if they didn't accept what they were offered?'

'Maybe some were,' Van Cole said, after thinking for a while. 'But most of those who sold out were offered a sum that was more than enough to make a new start in a place where an honest living was easier, with less trouble and better prospects.'

Mike, the waiter, returned. He gathered up their empty plates and offered them a selection of desserts. Everyone politely refused the desserts, but took refills on their coffees.

After several more minutes of conversation, Old Man Van Cole said as he left, 'Mrs. Smythe-Jones' family used to have a journal that her ancestors had kept from the founding until the beginning of the Great Depression. Might be some useful, or at least interesting, information in it.'

'I wonder if Julie knows about that

journal,' Jamie asked aloud after Old Man Van Cole walked out of the door. 'She's been close to the family most of her life. As Mr. Van Cole said, it could make for interesting reading.'

Sam agreed and offered to share what they had learned at the team meeting in the morning.

'This is beginning to seem as though someone feels that his people may have been cheated out of what he thinks should have been theirs.'

'But why not do it legally,' Jamie questioned, 'instead of through thievery, murder, and subterfuge?'

'Perhaps,' Sam answered with a thoughtful look, 'he believes that he is evidence gathering. I'm beginning to be just a bit curious about our Mr. 'Blue Man'. Age would have no bearing on hatred if he received it with his mother's milk.'

Sam and Jamie said their goodnights to Johanna and Mike as they left to go to their homes. When they reached the spaces where their cars were parked, Sam noticed what appeared to be a person asleep in a nearby doorway.

'He'll be safer if we wake him up and take him to a shelter for the night,' Jamie said.

'It's the right thing for two public-minded civil servants to do,' agreed Sam as they walked toward the man.

As they neared the man, they noted that he was bleeding. Jamie quickly knelt beside him as Sam called the emergency number.

'He's been slashed with a sharp knife,' Jamie reported to Sam as he talked to the dispatcher. 'He was assaulted and left here to either freeze or to bleed to death. He is too well dressed to be a homeless person.'

While Sam gave directions to their location and the details about what they found, Jamie began to triage the victim.

Sam brought a blanket from the trunk of his car and gave it to Jamie to keep the man warm as she worked to stop the bleeding.

'As soon as the paramedics arrive and are allowed to transport him to the hospital,' Jamie informed Sam, 'I'll ride with them and make sure that the ER people know everything that we know.'

'As soon as possible,' Sam nodded as he spoke, 'see if he has any identification on his person. I'll look around here for any clues while I wait for the forensics detail. Perhaps something will turn up that will help explain what happened.'

'You would think that someone would have given an alarm,' Jamie declared with a disappointed shake of her head.

'I'll have some patrol officers canvas the area,' Sam replied. 'Maybe someone who saw or heard something will be willing to tell us what they observed.'

The paramedics arrived first. By the time they had made sure that the man's vital signs were stable and that his wounds were no longer life threatening, Julie and Jack arrived along with the forensics detail and patrol officers, who swiftly cordoned off the scene. Forensics and Crime Scene Investigators quickly took their measurements, videoing and photographing the victim's position and his surroundings before the paramedics left for the hospital.

'Take a couple of officers and see if any

of the street people or patrons from the other businesses are willing to tell us anything,' Sam told them.

'There are still some civic-minded citizens who are willing to answer questions,' Jack commented. 'Maybe we'll get lucky and someone who knows something useful will be willing to help us.'

After his detectives left to see what they could find out, Sam began to search the area several yards away from where the victim was found, thinking that the man had made an attempt to escape his assailant, or assailants.

The parking lot outside of Johanna's had just been resurfaced and the lines designating the parking spaces had been repainted. Surely, some signs of a recent struggle would be noticeable in the freshness of the surface.

Squatting down to get a better look at the ground, near a lone vehicle parked about twenty feet from where the victim had been found, he saw something almost under the vehicle.

Taking out his pocket Mag-Lite flashlight, he shined it over the object that had caught his attention. In the light, it appeared to be a metal card case.

Calling to one of the forensics officers, he asked for surgical gloves and an evidence bag. Picking up what he found, he carefully opened it up. Then he dropped the card case into the evidence bag and used a marking pen to record where it had been found.

'This may have been dropped by the victim or the perp,' Sam theorized. 'I want this area marked off and the vehicle impounded. It's not likely that we have two crime scenes, but let's keep an open mind. A lost card case near an apparently abandoned vehicle near the scene of a crime makes me very suspicious. We'll need to check the business listed on the cards, too.'

'We'll have some extra portable lights set up and see what we can find before daylight,' the woman told him. 'We'll go over the place again after the sun comes up and try to finish our search before the businesses open up.'

★　★　★

Jonah Wilson AKA 'Blue Man', had returned to his rented apartment feeling satiated and ready to return to his 'borrowed' books and his notes. The only downside to his evening jaunt had been that nosey man in the parking lot. He had to have been a private cop sent by the psychiatric board and care clinic he had left several weeks ago. He knew he wasn't crazy. He was just seeking justice for himself and the others that had been cheated over a hundred years ago. The deputy mayor and his family had already paid for part of their corrupt activities with the death of the youngest male member. He had no idea if the private detective was dead or alive, but he didn't care right now. He wouldn't allow anyone to interfere in his affairs until he had completed what he had set out to do.

According to the histories of the earliest settlers and the recorded rainfall patterns, the wealthiest and most prestigious families were all descended from a small group of men from England, who had pooled their resources after liquidating their assets. A couple of men had come to the San Bernardino Mountains area, looking for inexpensive land where water could be cheaply piped in, or where there was a natural drainage area that could be made into viable farmlands with a few engineering changes.

After potable water was discovered under a 'dry lake' bed they had been considering, efforts were made to purchase as much of the acreage above the underground lake as possible.

The land was fertile, and, if properly irrigated by the underground lake, would prove to be exactly what the group was looking for: large enough for future growth, far enough away from the American influence to allow them to adapt their culture to their surroundings, but near enough to civilization for a healthy interaction of trade and ideas.

Ties to the mother country remained strong for several generations. So much so, that when the war in Europe began in 1914, a large group of young men joined the armed forces of Canada and Great Britain.

After the sinking of the *Lusitania*, and

the subsequent entry of the U.S. into the 'War to End All Wars', London, California offered land to the government for military grade weapons development and manufacture. A railway spur was added for the transportation of supplies and finished weapons. New industries came to the now burgeoning city and the city council began to look at ways to keep the water supply matching pace with the growing needs. Far-thinking plans were made and the city was in fair economic shape during the Great Depression.

The city had its ups and downs after the Second World War, but on average, was able to stay on a course of economic and cultural growth. By the beginning of the twenty-first century, London had nearly everything that could be found in any small-to-moderate-sized city: the Victorian Reading Room and library, the Lon-Cal *Times*, *The Midnight Confessor*, and radio and television stations that provided local, state, national, and international news. Movie houses, drive-ins, live theaters and opera houses provided entertainment and culture.

All of this, Jonah Wilson felt, was the due of the several families who had been convinced that their chances would be better somewhere else. His family patriarchs, in particular, had fallen upon hard times after being convinced by the silver-tongued investors that money in the hand *now* was better than staying on their dusty farmland with the pie in the sky promises of water being pumped up from the underground lake in future. His ancestors were convinced to accept a payment that was less than a third of its eventual worth. The family used the money to purchase a plot of land that looked good, but in reality had been overworked to the point of near-worthlessness.

The head of the family tried to work the land for several years before selling it at a loss and taking a factory job in a nearby city.

When the U.S. entered the 'Great War', the eldest son volunteered to fight. He came back, broken in health and bitter. He blamed the family misfortunes on the man who had convinced his father to sell his property. His children, grandchildren, and great-grandchildren were all told the story.

Jonah had tracked down several of the families from that time. Some told similar tales of woe and adversity while most had tales of gradual, even major, triumphs. Very few were as bitter as the Wilson family.

6

As Jamie rode to the hospital with the paramedics, the man being transported uttered the words 'found him' and then fell unconscious again. Jamie checked his vitals and found them steady, but weak.

'When we get back to the hospital,' the paramedics told her, 'we'll be able to match his blood type and begin to replenish his blood loss. While dangerous, his loss isn't critical. That was good work you did.'

'I once had to work on a patient while I was badly injured myself,' Jamie replied. 'I got a lot of practice slowing down the bleeding while waiting for the paramedics to arrive. The patient fully recovered after a long recuperation period.'

'Who was this fortunate person to have had you on call even when you needed doctoring yourself?' the paramedic wondered. 'Is there a chance of meeting him or her?'

'You already have,' Jamie grinned at him. 'He's the lieutenant who made the 911 call.'

★   ★   ★

The ER doctors worked quickly and efficiently on the man's injuries after he arrived.

'The man was lucky you and the lieutenant found him when you did,' one of the doctors informed her. 'By the time the next person to leave would have found him, he would have been in serious trouble, and with nobody with the proper training to give him emergency aid.'

'Was there any ID?' Jamie asked. 'Sam and I didn't have a chance to look.'

'His clothes and possessions are in the bin over by his bed,' she was told. 'Everything is just the way we removed them.'

Jamie had one of the orderlies witness what she found among the victim's collection of things. In his sport coat, she found an ID wallet identifying him as an operative working for J. Jameson Investigations in Sunnydale, Arizona. Jamie copied the phone number in her note-book. Next, she checked the shirt pockets and the front pants pockets and found nothing but a set of car keys for a hired vehicle from the local rental car agency.

When she checked a back pocket, she found a moderately priced leather wallet containing twenty five dollars, a VISA ATM card in the name of 'Andrew Monroe', an Arizona driver's license and an Arizona state-issued Private Investigator's license with the same name and a photograph that matched the victim.

'Now we have a name and a possible reason for the attack on him,' Jamie said triumphantly. 'I'll get to work on verifying this information. Sam and I didn't leave Johanna's all that long after the gentleman dressed in the blue denim suit.'

Sam heard Jamie's remarks as he entered the room and gave her a questioning look.

'What's that again, Jamie?'

'I'm wondering if our Mr. 'Blue Man' was being shadowed by our Mr. Andrew Monroe from Arizona,' she informed him. 'He appears to be a licensed PI and I was thinking that perhaps the two of them had an altercation in the parking lot while we were talking with Mr. Van Cole.'

'Anything's possible,' Sam replied. 'Coupled with the business card case I found almost under a car in the lot, the timing does make me suspicious. What else have you found out?'

'The surgeon found two stab wounds to the abdomen and a deep slash across the forehead,' Jamie replied. 'None of the wounds were immediately fatal, but if we hadn't found him when we did, he may have bled to death before anyone else found him. Our suspect may have had a motive, potentially had the opportunity, and there was definitely a method.'

The doctor came in to give his report and diagnosis.

'The victim has an excellent chance for recovery,' he reported. 'The knife wounds didn't puncture any vital organs or arteries and the slash to the forehead wasn't dangerous by itself, even though it bled profusely and barely missed the left eye.'

'Would you concur that the perpetrator

was right handed, Doctor?' Jamie wanted to know.

'From the way the wound was made,' the doctor agreed, 'I would say that the slice on the forehead was made from the victim's left side going to his right. That would normally indicate that the knife was wielded by a right-handed person facing his victim.'

'Mr. 'Blue Man' was definitely using his right hand when he was eating,' Sam observed. 'It may not be reason enough to ask some questions, but the timing definitely makes me want to know more about him.'

'Should we have Julie and Jack keep an eye on him?' Jamie asked.

'I think so, Jamie,' Sam said, 'but after you and Julie have had a chance to interview the Smythe-Joneses. See if Jonathan might have known our mystery man. I'll check with the Victorian Reading Room's employees and find out if anyone remembers him. I also want to place a twenty-four hour guard on Mr. Monroe. Someone evidently doesn't want him messing around in their business. That person may want to finish what he started when he learns that we found his victim, brought him here, and learned his name and occupation.'

'I agree,' Jamie said as she quickly looked at Monroe's chart. 'Private detectives don't usually get attacked in real life. What they are usually hired for doesn't normally involve violent people.'

The request was made and a uniformed officer was soon posted outside Andrew Monroe's door. The woman was a competent veteran officer with six years' experience on the force. Sam and Jamie both recognized her and felt that Mr. Monroe was in capable hands when they gave her instructions and the reasons behind them.

'Corporal Reid could be with one of the detective squads,' Jamie commented as they rode the elevator down to the ground floor lobby. 'Why is she still with the patrol units?'

'She likes getting home and being with her husband and kids in the evenings, but she doesn't mind taking special, short term assignments like this one periodically,' Sam replied. 'Corporal Reid claims these breaks in her routine make everyone appreciate when she's on her normal shift. A dependable routine at home is good for young children and her husband feels that she's safer with a reliable partner like Corporal Stevens.'

* * *

Jonah Wilson sat in the living area of his apartment thinking about the report he had heard on his police scanner the night before and the early morning report on the all-news radio station.

So, he thought, the man was found alive and appears to be recovering. Those two police detectives are lucky, meddling fools!

He slammed his fist on his knee in his frustration. 'Perhaps I was wrong not to worry about him,' he murmured to himself. 'Maybe I'll go pay a visit to the hospital and check up on 'my friend'. What could be more natural?'

* * *

Corporal Reid was going over the orders and events of her shift with her replacement, preparing to go home. Her children and husband soon would be heading out the door. She would just have time to kiss her family goodbye on their way to work and school.

As she headed down the hall, she observed a man in a blue denim outfit. She had seen him start up the hall when she was talking to Corporal Sorenson as she was getting ready to leave. He had turned around as if he had realized he was in the wrong hallway or, perhaps that he had forgotten something.

As she was about to push the elevator button, she remembered Sam's description of the man who was a person of interest. She reached for her radio and made a report to Sorenson.

'Person of Interest headed your way,' she said. 'Dressed in blue denim, slender build, middle years, average looking, no tell-tale marks, confident stride.'

'He's walking toward me,' Sorenson acknowledged.

'I'm calling for back up,' Reid answered,

'and I'm on my way back to you.'

Corporal Reid made her call for back up as she raced down the hall. As she reached Monroe's hospital room, she saw the man in blue standing over Sorenson's body with a knife that had a blade just long enough to be deadly. He had the knife raised for another plunge into the police officer.

'Freeze! Police!' she yelled at the man who turned, and quickly changing the knife's position in his hand, threw it in Reid's direction.

As she ducked away from the knife, she fired her service weapon. The bullet lodged itself in the wall just past her attacker as his knife barely missed her. The man in blue ran for the nearby fire stairs and vanished into the emergency exit.

Reid ran to Sorenson. She found him bleeding, but still alive. She made her reports of shots fired, officer down and in need of emergency aid, just as the elevator doors opened and an orderly, followed by one of the residents, came rushing down the hallway.

'We heard the shot!' the doctor said excitedly. 'We knew that there were officers posted on this floor. Is it safe for us to assist any injured?'

'Sorenson's been stabbed and he's bleeding badly,' Reid informed them. 'The suspect went out the fire stairs. I don't know if he went up or down.'

The doctor and the orderly immediately began working to stop the injured officer's blood loss.

The orderly, upon seeing blood on Reid's hands and clothing asked, 'Are you injured, Officer?'

Looking at herself, she told him that the blood wasn't hers, but from the other officer as she attempted to help him. The doctor got the bleeding under control and used his communication device to get a gurney to transport the man to an operating room for emergency surgery of his wounds.

Sam, Jamie, and several patrol officers came running down the hallway just as the doctor put away his communicator.

'"The Blue Man' was here,' Reid explained to Sam, 'but he got away when

I stopped to help Sorenson. He took the stairs, but I don't know if he went up or down.' Nervous reaction began to set in and Reid began to hiccup uncontrollably.

Jamie found a chair and sat her down and asked the orderly to bring some water. While he was getting the water, Jamie had Reid place her head between her knees and helped her control her breathing as she spoke in a soothing voice.

'Here, drink this,' Jamie said as the orderly handed her the paper cup of water that he had brought. 'Just take it in small sips and relax. You're okay and Sorenson is in the best care he could possibly get. Don't worry about 'Blue Man'. We'll catch him soon.'

Sam had the hospital security officers check with the nurses' stations to find out if their suspect had passed their way. No one had seen him; he had gotten away.

'I hate it,' Sam griped to himself, 'when a suspect just ups and disappears.'

★   ★   ★

'Our perp may decide that he needs to change his look after what happened,' Julie said at the next conference meeting. 'He was easily recognized by Corporal Reid last night and she warned Corporal Sorenson just before he was attacked.'

'He may not know how good a look Sam and I got of him,' Jamie remarked, 'or how good a witness Old Man Van Cole was during the sketch artist interview. The artist's rendering was photo perfect. I've never seen a sketch look so exact.'

'Do we go public with the sketch,' Jack questioned, 'or do we keep the information within the department for now?'

'Let's see what happens,' Sam said thoughtfully, 'as patrol officers work their beats and check their contacts. If they don't develop any leads for us in a couple of days, then we'll ask the general populace for help. I hope we can flush him out and keep him from going to ground.'

No further suggestions came to mind and the detectives began to leave their meeting.

'Julie,' Jamie stopped the woman as she was about to go out the door, 'did you want to drop by the Smythe-Jones' and show them the artist's sketch? Maybe they saw him and Jonathan together sometime.'

'It hasn't been a week yet,' Julie replied, 'but I don't think that there'll ever really be a good time to talk to them about Jonathan or his possible associates. Let's go now before I can change my mind.'

Jamie and Julie decided to drive Julie's vehicle to the Smythe-Jones' home.

'You know,' Julie said conversationally, trying to cover her nervous tension, 'Jonathan's family was one of the original families that homesteaded on the lake bed.'

'Did they homestead before or after the underground lake was discovered?' Jamie wondered.

'Oh, I think it was nearly five years before,' Julie said. 'There had been a co-op founded to create a canal that would bring water from one of the larger water sources for irrigation. After the underground water was found, the irrigation canal idea was abandoned and never finished. Jonathan's great-grandparents had claimed a very large parcel of land when they homesteaded. There were a few families who decided to try homesteading in other areas that appeared to have more promise before then. Some were given generous offers while others just walked away. Everyone who stayed made substantial profits after the water was found.'

'It sounds as if maybe some folks were able to really clean up if they knew ahead of time about the water,' Jamie remarked.

'Oh,' Julie responded, 'there were accusations made, but the courts didn't support any of the claims.'

'Maybe that's what our 'Blue Man' was looking for in those stolen books.'

As Jamie and Julie finished their conversation, they parked in the driveway of the Smythe-Jones' home and walked up to the front door.

The door was answered by Bobbie, the Smythe-Jones' daughter.

'Julie,' she said when she saw who was standing on the front porch. 'Please come in. You, too, Dr. Watson. Do you have anything new to tell us?'

'We have an artist's sketch of someone who may have more than a passing interest in the information in some books that have been stolen from the city's major libraries' rare book sections,' Jamie told her. 'He may also be involved in two attempted killings since Jonathan's death.'

'Do you know for sure that this is all related?'

'No,' Julie answered. 'One of the attempts was made on an out-of-state private investigator trying to find a psychiatric outpatient who has disappeared. The other attack severely injured the police officer guarding his hospital room. A Corporal Sorenson.'

Bobbie's face went pale and she started to collapse.

'Not *Thomas* Sorenson!' she gasped as Jamie and Julie caught her and helped her to a nearby chair. 'He proposed to me last night just as he was leaving for a special assignment!'

Bobbie's cries quickly brought a response from the rest of the family.

'Bobbie?' Mr. Smythe-Jones worriedly asked as he saw the ashen face of his daughter. 'What's happened?'

'Tom has been badly injured!' Bobbie wailed.

'Oh, no!' came from both Mrs. Smythe-Jones and Samantha. 'What happened?'

Jamie handed over the sketch and said, 'We think that this man may have been responsible for Jonathan's death as well as the attacks on a private investigator and Corporal Sorenson. Have any of you seen him? He apparently likes to wear blue denim suits.'

The members of the Smythe-Jones household all took long looks at the sketch, but no one recognized him.

The house phone rang and Samantha went to answer it. When she returned, she told Bobbie that the hospital had called.

'They said that Tom was out of danger. Before the operation and the sedatives and pain medication began to work, he was asking for you. According to the person on the phone, he really wants to see you when he wakes up. The doctors think it would be extremely helpful for you to be there.'

'We're done here,' Jamie said.

'Go. Be with your man,' Julie added. 'I'll check back later.'

7

Andrew Monroe was awake and had been asked if he felt up to talking to a couple of detectives.

'Yeah, go ahead and send 'em in,' he replied. 'You never know when you'll need a friend.'

Sam and Jack were led into the hospital room and introductions were made.

'Mr. Monroe,' Sam began, 'I was one of the two people who found you outside of Johanna's after you were attacked. What can you tell us about your attacker?'

'He's an outpatient from the Sunnydale Psychiatric Board and Care Facility,' Monroe told the two detectives. 'He was never considered dangerous. He just had this strong fixation about his family having been wrongfully made to leave their land and take some worn out, useless farmland when they moved. When he disappeared, the agency I work for was asked to find him and bring him back. They were concerned, that with his fixation, he might cause trouble for himself or others. When I saw him come out of that establishment, I stopped him. I told him who I was and why I wanted to talk to him. I asked him to return with me to the facility. Without any warning, he pulled out a knife and attacked me. The next thing I remember was waking up here.'

'While you were in recovery,' Jack informed him, 'a police officer assigned to protect you was brutally attacked and seriously injured. We believe he was attacked by the same man who attacked you.'

'The doctors in Sunnydale would be very interested in his change of behavior,' Monroe said. 'Up until he disappeared, he had never showed any violent tendencies. Not even when he was angry or annoyed.'

'What is the difference between an outpatient and an inmate?' Jack questioned.

'A facility outpatient lives on the grounds the same as an inmate, but has more freedom,' Monroe answered. 'Both are under 24/7 supervision, but an outpatient can earn passes to leave the facility under supervision. Jonah Wilson was on a forty-eight hour pass to see the sights in nearby Yuma, when his attendant lost sight of him. Notification was made to the facility and the authorities made a quiet search. When word came that Jonah had last been seen boarding a bus for California, my agency was hired to track him down and bring him back. It was then believed that he could cause annoyance, or trouble, for the people he blamed for his family's impoverishment and embarrassment to the facility. But, as I said, no one really thought that he would become vicious or violent.'

'Perhaps we need to send for his therapist,' Sam suggested. 'Would Sunnydale be willing to send someone out here to consult?'

'If Jonah has turned violent,' Monroe added, 'you'll need all the help you can get in making up his new profile, and quickly!'

*   *   *

Bobbie arrived at the hospital and told the front desk who she was and who she wished to see.

'I was told that he asked to see me just before his operation,' she said.

'He's still asleep and resting comfortably,' the resident informed her. 'He should be waking up soon. He'll probably be groggy from the meds and have some pain, but you should be able to see him for a few minutes. If you're family, you can wait by his bedside until he wakes.'

'We're *almost* family,' Bobbie told her, her eyes glistening with unshed tears. 'He proposed to me just before he went on shift. I haven't had a chance to give him an answer yet.'

'If the answer is the one he's hoping for, I think that would be better than any medicine that I can give him,' the resident smiled. 'He's young, healthy, and strong. His chances of recovery have been considered good, but I think they may have just been raised to excellent.'

Bobbie quietly entered Sorenson's room after the resident had hospital security place her on the approved visitors' list.

'Tom,' she whispered, her voice tremulous from holding back her tears, 'please wake up. I want to tell you how much you mean to me and that I'd be proud to be your wife and have your children.'

Bobbie saw his lips twitch in the beginning of a smile as his eyes slowly opened and then focused on her.

'Was I dreaming,' he questioned, 'or did I really hear you say that you'd marry me?'

'You heard me,' Bobbie answered, as she got closer to the bed and leaned over to lightly kiss his lips. '"To have and to hold until death do us part". But let's hold off for a long time on the parting thing, OK?'

'You've got my wholehearted agreement, light of my life,' Sorenson grinned.

They both were laughing as the duty nurse arrived with a tray of bandages.

'Oh, good,' she said as she let her presence be known. 'You're awake and in a good mood. If your lady-friend would step outside for a few minutes while I check your stitches and change your bandages, the two of you can continue your conversation. I'll let the doctor know that you're awake.'

Bobbie went to the hallway to await the finish of the nurse's administrations.

The nurse checked Sorenson's monitors and vital signs and then began to gently unwrap the old bandages. The wounds showed no signs of infection and the monitors all gave normal readings. The nurse talked as she worked.

'Your lady-friend seems nice,' the nurse told him as she applied a new antiseptic dressing over his wounds. 'I presume that you have had the talk with her that you wanted?'

'Yes, we did,' he answered. 'She said that she would be honored, so now I just need to get well enough to leave here so that we can make our wedding plans.'

'Wonderful!' the nurse enthused as she rewrapped his bandages. 'I wish the two of you a long and happy life together.'

The nurse finished and then disposed of the old bandages. As she left the room, she smiled at Bobbie.

'It sounds like the two of you have a lot to talk about,' she said. 'Don't tire him out, though. Physical trauma can be very exhausting. The doctor should arrive soon. I'm going to let him know Corporal Sorenson's status as soon as I see him. At any rate, he should be here as soon as he makes his rounds.'

'I won't let him overextend himself, Nurse,' Bobbie let her know. 'I want him healthy as soon as possible and around for a long time.'

* * *

'Doesn't it seem odd to you,' Jack questioned as he and Sam walked back to his car, 'that a psychiatric patient, no matter how apparently stable he or she seems, and who is required to live on the facility's grounds, should have the freedoms that have been described by Mr. Monroe?'

'Yes, it does.' Sam rubbed his chin thoughtfully. 'Either the Arizona Psychiatric Board's rules are more lax than ours, or the facility is bordering on criminal

94

negligence. This case is turning out to have interesting implications.'

'Why don't I check with the Arizona licensing board and find out what I can about the Sunnydale facility. Maybe there have been other problems or complaints made in the past.'

'That sounds good, Jack.' Then Sam added, 'Check with Jamie on ethics and rules of behavior. As a licensed medical practitioner, she would more likely to be up to date than you or I.'

Both men drove back to the station, each wrapped up in their own private thoughts.

'What have Julie and I gotten ourselves into?' Jack questioned himself. Sam and Jamie had gotten a reputation for receiving odd and/or difficult cases. Both had been on fast track paths before Captain Reynolds had paired them together on what had become known as the Super-TASER case. Sam and Jamie's experiences had led to some spirited discussions of personal procedural protocols between him and Julie about their roles and how they worked together. They had once again agreed to let the situation itself determine which of them took point during dangerous engagements. Jack's sense of chivalry didn't always agree with a hurried decision made under duress, but he readily acknowledged that Julie had saved his life as often as he had saved hers.

Sam was just getting used to having a partner he fully trusted to watch his back. Now he was responsible for an entire team. 'No pressure,' Lieutenant Baker had told him, 'just trust your instincts and your training.' But right now he wished for the old days when he and Jamie had first started working together.

Their musings ended as Jack pulled into the police parking lot. The two men went to the departmental cafeteria. The coffee carafe had been allowed to go empty and was sitting in the sink.

'Looks like we've got a choice of a cold beverage from the vending machine or making a new pot of coffee,' Jack said resignedly. 'What do you say?'

Sam looked at his watch. 'I think that it's close enough to the end of watch so that we can go home and grab a bite. Then I'll review my notes on the case for a while. There's not much more we can do here tonight. We'll tackle this in the morning when we're fresh.'

Julie and Jamie walked into the cafeteria. Julie looked at the empty carafe in the sink.

'What?' she sighed, greatly disappointed. 'No coffee, *again*!'

'Johanna's is within walking distance,' Jamie suggested. 'Her coffee is better than the brew served here. Besides, I'm hungry and I don't feel like nuking something from the freezer in my apartment.'

'That sounds great to me,' the others agreed simultaneously.

The walk to Johanna's was uneventful and the atmosphere was warm and welcoming. Sam and Jamie saw that their usual booth in the back corner was occupied. Mike, the head waiter, informed them that another booth had just been made available and led them to a large booth that would have easily seated twice their number.

'This will be fine, Mike,' Sam grinned.

'I'll start with coffee, black.'

Jack, Julie, and Jamie each ordered beverages and Mike left menus for everyone. While he catered to other customers, Julie sipped from her cup of sweet and light coffee, and then said, 'Did anyone know that Tom Sorenson and Bobbie Smythe-Jones were involved with each other?'

Sam and Jack shook their heads as Julie continued. 'It seems that just before he was called to stand post at the hospital, he proposed to Bobbie. He said that he was willing to wait for her answer since he had to leave before she could give her reply. She was hit pretty hard by our news. Fortunately, the hospital called just then with the news that Sorenson was out of danger and that he had said he wanted to see her as soon as he could.'

'We had shown 'Blue Man's' sketch to the family before the hospital called, but no one recognized him,' Jamie added.' We let Bobbie go to the hospital to be with Sorenson and returned to the station.'

'I remember Tom from his first day as a new recruit fresh from the academy,' Jack remarked. 'He was the first rookie that I was partnered with after I had made full patrol officer. I thought that he showed a lot of promise.'

'His record proves that you were right,' Julie added. 'He should make detective soon, if he wants to go in that direction with his carrier. If events continue down the path they're headed, he may decide to do just that.'

★   ★   ★

Andrew Monroe lay in his hospital bed reviewing the things he had been told and the events that had transpired after he had found, and then approached, Wilson. Nothing in Wilson's files or profile had prepared him for the vicious and unprovoked attack. He had been reported as verbally volatile, but physically harmless.

What had happened to have made such a major change in his personality?

While Monroe pondered these questions, and others, the nurses and his doctor came in and checked on his continuing recovery.

Bobbie saw Corporal Reid coming down the hall toward Sorenson's room. Reid stopped, looked at Bobbie and asked, 'Do you know Officer Sorenson? You look familiar.'

'Yes, I do,' Bobbie said, and then asked a question of her own. 'Who are you?'

'Officer Janice Reid,' was her reply. 'I tried to warn Tom about our perpetrator. Now, please tell me how you know Tom.'

Bobbie related the details about Tom's proposal of marriage, how Julie and Jamie had come to her family's home with questions and a sketch of the man they believed to be implicated in her brother's death and how the news had inadvertently precipitated her near collapse, and the call from the hospital, letting her know that Tom was out of danger and that he had asked to see her.

'You must be Bobbie,' Reid commented. 'I remember him talking about someone special with that name. I think that I have seen you with him when he was off duty a few times. How is he doing?'

'The doctors are expecting a full recovery. He just fell asleep.'

'Would you let him know that I stopped by and asked about him?' Reid inquired. 'And please let him know that all of his friends in the department are praying and sending good thoughts and best wishes for his quick recovery.'

'I will,' Bobbie agreed. 'I certainly don't want to lose him now.'

8

The administrators of the Sunnydale Psychiatric Board and Care Facility went into full 'cover your butt' mode when they were told about Jonah Wilson's escapades since he had lost his watchers. The two main questions on their minds were 'How did he slip away from our surveillance team?' and 'How was he able to hide his violent tendencies?' Hours had been spent trying to figure the best way to spin-doctor the situation. Obviously, he was much better at manipulating his doctors than anyone had given him credit for.

'Two of London, CA's best detectives are driving here to get a profile on Wilson,' the head administrator, a late middle-aged man dressed in a low-priced but fancy tailored suit, informed his staff. 'If they believe that we've been negligent or incompetent, they could appeal to the Arizona State licensing board to shut us down. The slightest breath of scandal could do irreparable damage to our reputation.'

'Up until now, Doctor Kindle,' began another administrator, who closely resembled the usual stereotype of a psychiatrist, 'we have had a sterling reputation and excellent results from our treatment methods. Surely, this Wilson's actions can't affect us *that* badly.'

'According to the report from J. Jameson Investigations,' a woman administrator in a tailored jacket and skirt and wearing nicely appointed jewelry spoke up, 'Wilson may have killed one man, and wounded one of their men, as well as a police officer, and stolen several rare and historically important books. I think that, yes, Mr. Wilson's actions can, and probably will, hurt this facility. The only questions are, 'How soon?' and 'How badly?''

'All right,' Dr. Kindle responded. 'Pull every file we have generated and every scrap of information that we've received from anyone who has ever treated Jonah Wilson. It will all have to be thoroughly reviewed by the time that Lt. Holmes and

Dr. Watson arrive, late tomorrow afternoon.'

The administrators looked at each other for an extremely brief moment, and then hurried out to gather the needed records.

★   ★   ★

At a filling station outside of Needles, Sam and Jamie stopped to fill the gas tank of Sam's personally owned vehicle and to stretch their legs.

'The Arizona border isn't much further,' Jamie commented as the muscles, tendons, and bones in her back all snapped and popped as she stretched her body first left, and then right, several times. 'This is a longer drive than the one to Las Vegas to see my brother and his family. I'm glad that we took your car instead of one of the unmarked vehicles. You've got more leg room and more comfortable seats.'

'I figured that since the department wasn't paying for this trip, we may as well ride in comfort,' answered Sam. 'Besides, my car needs a workout now and then.'

'Do we have time to have a cold glass of tea or a Coke?' asked Jamie. 'It must be a hundred and ten degrees in the shade around here.'

'As soon as we fill the tank,' agreed Sam, 'we'll see what that attached eatery has to offer.'

They entered the fast-food/diner combination and found an empty table by the window toward the back that also gave a good view of customers as they entered the place.

'This place could have come from an early post-war movie about a small town,' Sam observed.

'Or even one of those early alien monster invasion flicks,' Jamie agreed.

The sixty-something waitress heard these comments as she approached their table.

'This diner was used in several grade-B horror flicks back in the late fifties and the early sixties,' she commented as she set menus down in front of her customers. 'Can I get you folks something to drink while you decide on your order?'

Jamie smiled and asked, 'Do you have iced tea available? It's very hot outside, and I'm feeling dehydrated.'

'I'll have the same,' Sam added.

'Would you like lemon with your tea?' the helpful waitress inquired as she made a note in her ticket book. Seeing the negative shakes of their heads, the waitress added when she returned with two frosted mugs, 'This place was a featured set in 'The Glob vs. the Monster from Grey Canyon'. I got absorbed by the Glob in one scene. My fifteen seconds of fame.'

'That little girl was you?' Jamie exclaimed. 'I was really young when it was shown on the Late Night Movie Show on television. My folks didn't know that I had sneaked out of bed to watch it until I started screaming, 'Don't let it eat me! Mommy, Daddy, don't let it get me!' How did they get you to do that scene and not give you bad dreams for the rest of your life?

'I was told that everything was a pretend game by my parents and grandparents. The director even showed me how the rubber Glob monster was worked by wires and pulleys. Then, I was allowed to play inside it for an hour or so before they shot the scene. I don't know that very many people saw that film. Even for a summer, date-night flick, it was a flop. My grandparents, who owned and ran the diner back then, liked having the extra income the diner brought when the studios from Hollywood used it in one of their movies. Usually, my parents wouldn't let me near the place when they were shooting horror flicks. They said that they were lucky with that one film and they didn't want me to begin having night terrors or the 'screaming willies'.'

'Did you ever have traumatic fears from the experience, or unexplained phobias?' Sam questioned.

'Only once,' the senior citizen claimed. 'My dad told me that, when I had just turned six, we went to the diner to help my grandparents. A man had brought in some still shots from that film and had them laid out on the counter. They looked pretty realistic after the FX people had finished. I had never seen the finished product, so these stills were quite a shock. I didn't recognize my then four-year-old self and I just stared at the little girl being swallowed by this gigantic mass of goo. My dad saw the pictures on the counter and quickly gathered me up in his arms; telling me that everything was all right, that the person taking the pictures was using the camera to make imaginary things to look at. He explained how that often, in the movies, film could be used to make pretend things look like they were real, because they couldn't really happen, or that they were too dangerous to film if they were real. Then he asked me if I knew the child in the photographs. When I said 'no,' he explained that it was me when I was much younger and that since nothing bad had happened to me, the little girl was playing a game and that no one really got swallowed up. I just helped the cameraman make pretend pictures.'

Later, when Sam and Jamie had finished and were driving away, Jamie remarked, 'That was certainly an interesting story that waitress told us. How much do you think was true?'

'I think most of it was,' Sam offered, 'at least from the way she remembers it. Do you happen to remember the name on her nametag?'

'Janey, wasn't it?'

'There was a Jane Atfield listed on Google as a former outpatient at the Sunnydale Psychiatric Board and Care Facility,' Sam observed. 'At our next stop with a Wi-Fi connection, see if you can find a complete list of actors and extras for that film.'

★ ★ ★

'The detectives from California have arrived, Dr. Kindle,' the thirtyish and statuesque secretary announced.

'Show them in, Sandra,' Dr. Kindle said, quickly straightening his desk. 'And please see that they have refreshments. After all, they have had a long drive.'

'Dr. Kindle will see you now,' Sandra told them, and then asked, 'Would you care for something to drink? I'm sure that you must be hot and thirsty after driving all the way from California.'

109

'We're fine,' Jamie answered, standing up.

'We stopped just outside of Needles for gas,' Sam added as he also got up from his seat. 'There was an interesting, and unique, diner next door. The waitress and owner had some interesting stories to tell about its history.'

Sandra gave Sam and Jamie quick, puzzled looks before taking them back to Dr. Kindle's office. With a professional smile — one that showed his perfectly cared for teeth, but did not reflect in his eyes — Dr. Kindle came around his sturdy, but unpretentious, desk and said, as he offered his hand to the detectives, 'Welcome. I understand that you may have found our missing patient.'

'We've been reliably informed that a person of interest, and possible suspect, in the thefts of several out-of-print volumes of historical significance, one homicide, and three assaults, may have had a connection with this facility,' Sam said without a show of emotion.

'DNA found at the site of the homicide is inconclusive at this time,' Jamie added.

'However, other forensic and eyewitness evidence seems to indicate that all of the crimes were committed by the same person.'

'I can understand calling Lt. Holmes a detective, and his interest in the case,' Dr. Kindle stated softly, 'but I'm not sure that I understand the involvement of a medical doctor, nor why a MD should be rated as a detective.'

'My full credentials are *MD, FME*,' Jamie replied. 'One of my primary duties as a forensic medical examiner is to document all forensic evidence at the scene of a homicide and thereby give the pathologists possible clues to look for in an autopsy. My training at Johns Hopkins Hospital and experience at the Medical Examiner's and Coroner's divisions of the LPD have involved all sorts of medical detective work. Lt. Holmes and I have been teamed up on several difficult cases. Surely, as a psychiatrist, you've been involved in a bit of detective work in diagnosing a patient?'

'I've never looked at my work from that aspect before, Dr. Watson.' Dr. Kindle's brow wrinkled in thought at what was to him, a new idea. 'Maybe I should.'

'Without breaking patient confidentiality, Dr. Kindle,' Sam began the interview in earnest, 'what can you tell us about Jonah Wilson?'

'What do you already know, or think you know, about this patient?' the doctor inquired. 'If you already have knowledge of certain facts, I may be able, ethically, to verify or challenge your assumptions or conclusions. As you say, death and serious injury has already occurred, and there is reason to assume that more of the same is possible.'

'A Google search of Jonah Wilson has indicated background for a motive behind his alleged actions. Also, an interview with a person who had at least one lengthy conversation with Jonah Wilson AKA 'Blue Man', points to a strong, possibly unhealthy, interest in the actions and events during the time of the water-witching that discovered the water under the site being homesteaded that became the city of London, CA. The nickname was given to identify a man who always wore blue denim suits, but did not give his name. Corroborating evidence has made it clear that this is the same man.

'An operative hired to return Wilson was attacked without obvious provocation. He did serious bodily harm to the operative. The operative, when allowed by the doctors to speak with us, gave us information that led us here. Wilson has been implicated in the death of one of our citizens, the theft of irreplaceable books from several of our libraries, and attacks on at least two of our city's guardians.

'Our information also states that Wilson, while under your facility's care, gave no indication of hostile or violent tendencies. We are aware that Wilson has a fixation about his family having been forced, by unfair and possibly illegal actions to give up their rights to property that could have made them wealthy, if they had known about the water under the dry lakebed.'

'Until the possibly accidental death of the deputy mayor's son, Wilson may have just been interested in the books as evidence of wrongdoing by some of our city fathers. Could Smythe-Jones' death have unbalanced his mind to the point where he could have become capable of planned homicide?'

Dr. Kindle rubbed his chin as he gave himself time to organize his thoughts into something that would be true, and yet undamaging to his own reputation, or to that of the facility he had helped found, for being unethical or negligent.

'Patient Wilson had been recommended to us by his physician for treatment of slight sleep disturbance and anxiety disorders. His therapy and treatment programs were reported to be progressing toward a healthy resolution along a normal, and expected, path. As a reward, he was allowed a forty-eight hour sightseeing and shopping trip to Yuma.

'Within a few hours of his arrival in Yuma with his certified psychiatric attendant, he disappeared in a crowded shopping mall next to the local Museum of Natural and Cultural History. The authorities had to be alerted of course, and they were soon able to trace his movements to the long distance bus station where he bought a one-way ticket to California.'

'Where did he get the funds for the ticket?' Jamie wanted to know. 'And what is the main difference between those that I heard referred to as 'inmates' and those called 'outpatients'. Aren't outpatients those who are treated and go home to recuperate after treatment? Yet I understand that both groups live here at the facility.'

'An 'inmate' is a person who has broken with reality and needs to be locked away to prevent harm to themselves or others. These patients are provided with 24/7 on-site emergency therapy and medical care and are constantly under guard. 'Outpatient' is really a misnomer. This is a person who is still in touch with reality, and can potentially regain his or her equilibrium with society. Such a person, under proper supervision, can be given small doses of interaction, such as visits to museums, shopping malls, and may even have pets here at the facility.

'An 'outpatient' can have debilitating anxieties or such deep rooted fixations that they need constant supervision, but are still able to enjoy outings such as the one that Wilson was given. As for where his funds came from, he seems to have had a bank account that was supposed to provide for his medical and therapy treatments but which was not under a trusteeship. This was not the way it was supposed to have been done.'

'And what about this seeming change from harmless, but possibly annoying fixation to violent reactions to perceived interference with his plans and goals, Doctor?' Sam queried.

'My theory,' Dr. Kindle answered, 'is that something has triggered a psychotic break and a major shift in personality.'

'Something like schizophrenia?'

'Not quite like that,' Dr. Kindle said after pondering the question. 'More like a deeply hidden anger that has now been allowed full control of Wilson's psyche. I believe that he is now unpredictable and most likely dangerous, if he feels thwarted or threatened.'

'How could he have kept all of this hidden from his therapists?' Jamie asked. 'Wasn't there any indication of what may have been happening?'

'The human mind is a quite complex, and largely unknown, territory, Dr. Watson,' she was answered. 'Even the most intuitive and insightful mental health professional can be taken in by a skillful bull-artist. No one is telepathic, nor can anyone sense another's emotions.'

After this interview, Sam and Jamie were given permission to conduct interviews with Wilson's therapists, nurses, and his certified psychological attendant.

These interviews, and a visit to Wilson's room, were concluded much too late to start back to California. The motel still had two rooms available and Sam and Jamie both left requests for early wake-up calls the next day.

Sam called Lt. Baker from his cell phone and gave him a progress report. 'Our suspect should be considered extremely dangerous, possibly armed, and very devious. He should be approached only with utmost caution and absolute necessity. Everyone we interviewed agreed that he no longer has the same personality as before he left Arizona.'

After Sam had switched off his cell phone, he and Jamie discussed whether or not to stop again at the diner in Needles.

'The Google search is what gave us the lead that Janey was once a patient at the Sunnydale Psychiatric Board and Care Facility.' Jamie was insistent that it may not be in the waitress' best interest to question her about her past at the facility. 'We don't know what hidden fears may be brought out in the open.'

'Yes,' agreed Sam, 'but if we are careful and go slow, we may also get a better insight as to the nature of the facility's therapeutic value.'

9

Jamie was bothered by the breach of confidentiality that the Google search had revealed: the identity of a former patient at Dr. Kindle's facility. Even if no details of the treatment were involved, the broken trust in the doctor and patient relationship could have permanently devastating results. It was apparent that Jamie wished to place that episode in her investigative life behind her.

An information search of the names of all of the participants from the old monster film did not bring up any girl called 'Jane' or 'Janey' as the young girl who had the role as one of the Glob's victims. Children who had bit parts in the movies back then were often given stage names, or referred to in some other way.

'I'm wondering if, at the time,' Jamie told Sam, 'her parents and grandparents got the studio to suppress her part in the film. Look at their efforts to keep her away from the crews that came later.'

'The story about her reactions to those stills of her and the monster is, perhaps, more telling than even she is aware of,' Sam agreed. 'Did Google give the date that Jane Atfield was at Sunnydale?'

'No,' Jamie answered, 'but if she was having night terrors, or episodic anxiety, or panic attacks, she could have been any age. At any rate, I don't believe she was admitted voluntarily.'

'Okay, Jamie,' Sam said, 'we'll go ahead with our planned stop in Needles for gas and lunch and let the conversation follow her lead.'

★   ★   ★

Sam and Jamie stopped at the gas station and diner in the early afternoon. As Sam filled the gas tank, Jamie talked to the station attendant.

'Do you know how long the current owner of the diner next door has run it?' she asked the man, who was in his early forties.

'She was here when I bought this

station fifteen years ago,' he smiled. 'The man I bought it from when he retired told me that it had been run by three generations of the same family. Janey loves to regale people passing through of its movie days. There used to be poster-sized pictures of how the place looked in some of those old films.'

'I didn't notice any pictures when my friend and I were here the last time,' she told the attendant. 'Do you know what happened to them?'

'I heard that they were all up one day then gone the next. Nobody knows why.' The man shrugged his shoulders. 'Even with the pictures gone, Janey seems to love those memories'

Sam finished filling his tank and walked over to pay for the gasoline.

'Ready for something to eat?' he asked Jamie.

'Yes, sweetheart,' she replied in the code that let Sam know that she had some private information for him. 'I'm starved. That continental breakfast at the motel this morning didn't seem to stay with me.'

121

' "Breakfast is the most important meal of the day',' Sam quoted. 'That's why one should never skip or scrimp on it. It sets the tone for the rest of the day.'

'Sometimes,' Jamie returned, 'one has no choice and must make do.'

'All too true. Let's go get some sustenance.'

As they entered the empty diner, Sam and Jamie were greeted by the smiling owner.

'Welcome back,' she said waving them into the seating area. 'You're a bit early for the midday rush. Take a seat wherever you want.'

Sam guided Jamie to a booth in the back next to the window. From there, they had a complete view of the parking lot and the gas station, as well as the dining room.

'That was a quick trip,' Janey said as she set the breakfast and lunch menus before her customers. 'Did you find what you were looking for?'

'Yes and no,' Sam replied. 'We got some information and a few answers to some questions. We just haven't figured out how helpful all of it is yet.'

'I've lived within a hundred to two hundred miles of here all of my life and I've run this diner for almost thirty years since my parents moved to Montana.'

'Did you parents take over from your grandparents?' Jamie inquired.

'Only for about five years.' Janey seemed glad for the company of newcomers and the opportunity to talk. 'My grandparents tried to sell the diner and retire, but were unable to find a buyer willing to keep its historic looks and atmosphere.'

The Greyhound bus drove into the area between the gas station and the diner. The driver and about a dozen people got out. The driver informed his passengers that they would have forty-five minutes to eat, stretch their legs, and take care of anything else while the vehicle's fuel tank was filled. He also told Janey to have the cook prepare his usual.

The driver went back outside and drove the bus over to the diesel fuel pumps and placed the nozzle into the fill pipe.

Janey and another waitress began distributing menus and taking orders.

'If the bus line makes regular stops here,' Sam observed as Janey had placed their orders on the cook's order wheel, 'perhaps someone remembers our suspect.'

'I wonder if he was wearing his blue denim suit by then?' Jamie wondered. 'That could be a better memory jogger than the sketch.'

Sam shrugged as their meals were placed before them.

By the time they were leisurely finishing their meals and getting their drinks refilled, the crowd was thinning out and returning to the bus. The driver had gotten off of his stool at the counter and announced to those who were still in the diner that he would be pulling out in ten minutes.

'Now we get a breather until people start getting off at the end of the normal work day,' Janey said as she sat down in a chair at a nearby table. 'Anna, Rog, and I have a chance to rest our feet for a few minutes.'

'Perhaps, while you're resting,' Sam said, seizing his opportunity, 'you could help us. I've got a sketch of someone that may have come through here on the bus about a month ago.'

As Sam retrieved the folded sketch of Jonah Wilson, he and Jamie both pulled out their badges and ID wallets. 'We think that this man may have left the Sunnydale Psychiatric Board and Care Facility and is now in London, CA. We believe that he may have information about, or have been involved in, some things that we would like to clear up.'

'I wish that I could forget about that place,' Janey said in a hushed voice. 'Mom and Dad put off their move to Montana because of my being in that place.'

Sam and Jamie gave each other a look of surprise at these unexpected, and voluntary, statements. The anguish in Janey's voice was heartbreaking.

Janey seemed to gather herself together, took a deep breath and then continued. 'I had gone to Yuma to find a present for my parents' anniversary. I was told later that I had started crying and running in circles, terrified. I kept trying to escape the crowds and would change directions when anyone tried to approach me. I finally collapsed from nervous exhaustion. That's when I was talked into a closed vehicle and taken to Sunnydale.

'After seventy-two hours, my parents were able to get the police to begin a missing person's search for me. When I was found at the facility, my parents were told that there had been no way of identifying who I was or who to contact. My parents told me that when they were finally allowed to see me, I appeared to be drugged and unable to recognize them. I went through years of mental hell, not knowing truth from fantasy because of their 'therapy'.

'My parents finally secured my release from the Sunnydale facility and I spent the next three years working here and making weekly, and then monthly, trips to a psychologist here in Needles. The routine and responsibilities were part of her recommended therapy for me. She told me that a constant, but variable, routine and responsibilities would be a stabilizing factor to me.

'I finally progressed to the point where my psychologist agreed to let me make appointments on an 'as needed' basis.

'My parents and I sought restitution. What we received was only enough to keep the diner out of bankruptcy and pay the lawyer's fees while I went through my 'rehabilitation therapy' after my release from Sunnydale.'

'What you've just told us,' Jamie replied, 'may help us understand our 'Blue Man'.'

'Did you happen to see him?' Sam asked quietly.

'No, but he may have come through on the late bus after my night manager came on duty,' Janey replied. 'He comes on at six. We both work twelve-hour shifts.'

'Our man has been known as a big tipper,' Sam informed her as he left the sketch. 'That may help your night manager and crew remember him. If anyone does remember anything, please call one of the numbers on our cards. It may be important to our investigation.'

★　★　★

'What Janey told us about her time in the Sunnydale facility,' Jamie commented as they drove back home, 'doesn't sound ethical to me. I think that she may have been involuntarily used as a human experiment and probably held against her will. I wonder why the settlement wasn't more. It almost sounds as if the facility paid someone to keep things quiet, while limiting their financial liability.'

'That would go a long way toward keeping themselves away from a licensing investigation,' Sam agreed. 'I wonder how much they may have cleaned up their act and how much better they may be hiding their current actions.'

'One thing's for sure,' Jamie replied, 'we really need to find Jonah Wilson and have a trusted professional sit down with him.'

★　★　★

Julie and Jack were at their desks going over the files on the library thefts and the homicide and homicide attempts when Lt. Baker walked over to their desks.

'There's a lot of pressure from the Commissioner's and the Mayor's offices for a speedy solve on this one,' he said without preamble. 'Can you give me a positive update for Captain Reynolds, so he can keep the powers that be off of your backs while the four of you work without your elbows being jostled every ten minutes?'

Jack looked at Julie and a silent signal went between them that let him know that he was to give the answer.

'Sam and Jamie are checking on some information about the facility our suspect was staying at before he eluded their custody in Yuma, Arizona.' Jack was in full report mode. 'They both feel that there were things going on there that need an in-depth look.'

'Jamie felt that our suspect's case may have been mishandled,' Julie added.

'They called me yesterday,' Baker told them, 'to tell me that they would be back sometime today. If you should see them before I do, let them know that the Captain and I want a verbal report immediately upon their return. I'll also leave word on their desk computers.'

With his message delivered, Lt. Baker went back to his office and began to check the reports of the other detectives under him.

Julie was about to say something to Jack when her desk phone rang. She listened for several moments, wrote down some quick notes, and placed the receiver back in its cradle.

'Mr. Monroe just went into respiratory arrest,' she said as she grabbed her purse and her jacket. 'Just before his attack, a male nurse who wasn't on the list, but who showed the proper authorizations, was admitted into his room. Just minutes after the nurse left, the monitors began sending out alarms.'

Jack and Julie arrived at the hospital five blocks away in record time and were admitted quickly onto the floor where the private detective was. The officer on duty told them that the doctors were working on the patient and no one was allowed access until the okay was given.

'All I know is that after the male nurse left,' the detectives were told, 'the monitor alarms started yowling, the code blue announcement was blaring over the intercom, and all hell broke loose on the floor.'

Jack took a copy of the 'Blue Man' sketch from his jacket pocket.

'Is this the male nurse you let into Mr. Malone's room before his episode?' he asked.

The officer in charge of Andrew Monroe's security took a long look at the proffered sketch.

'Yeah, it looks like it could have been him,' he said, handing it back. 'I had been informed that some guy who liked wearing blue denim outfits had already tried to off the patient in the room I was supposed to watch, but no one had shown me a picture. Besides that, he had all of the right papers and he was wearing those green nursing scrubs everyone wears around here.'

'What can you tell us about the suspect?' Julie asked, taking out her notebook.

'I did notice that his eyes were an odd color,' the guard remarked after a moment's contemplation. 'They had the color of a rotten walnut shell. The pupils had almost no contrast. Sorta like the mounted head of deer my uncle had on the wall of his game room. You know, kinda glassy.'

'Do you mean like a blank stare?' the detective sergeant wondered.

'No, he blinked too fast for that,' she was answered. 'It more like there was nothing behind those eyes.'

'Okay.' Julie closed her note book. 'If you remember, or you think of anything, give a call to the Robbery-Homicide Division and tell them that it's about the case Lt. Holmes is working on. Understand?'

'Gotcha.'

Julie turned to her partner and gave a head nod as they took a few steps down the hall.

'I'll wait here until the crash team is through,' she told Jack. 'Pass out copies of that sketch at the nurses' stations on a couple of floors and see if anyone knows of a male nurse with a habitual 'thousand yard stare'.'

'That does sound like what the guard was describing, doesn't it?' Jack observed. 'That eye color description sounds creepy, too.'

The crash team came out of the room, looking grim, but relieved. The lead physician motioned the others to return the crash cart where it belonged for replenishing as he stripped off his surgical gloves and walked toward the guard and the detectives.

'The patient is stable,' he reported, 'but it was touch and go for several minutes. Fortunately, his monitors alerted the nursing station in time for a quick-thinking nurse to change the IV bag in case of contamination or tampering. The patient soon began to rally, and after we gave him a broad-spectrum injection of anti-toxins, all of his vital signs slowly but steadily returned to normal.'

'Was the IV bag saved for analysis?' Julie inquired. 'We have reason to believe that this was a direct attempt on Mr. Monroe's life.'

The doctor used his communicator to check on the status of the IV bag. With a frown, he told the detectives, 'Unfortunately, in the confusion of the emergency, the bag has already been placed in the hazardous waste disposal. It's standard operating procedure to . . . '

'We understand,' Jack interrupted. 'Is there any way to find out what was used as a poison?'

'Not very likely after the large dose of anti-toxin we administered.' The doctor shook his head in regret. 'We had to be very careful not to give him an overdose and cause problems at the other end of the spectrum. All of the toxins in his system will have been neutralized by now.'

Julie and Jack thanked the doctor and returned to the police station.

⋆　⋆　⋆

Sam and Jamie pulled into the station just as Julie and Jack were getting out of their car.

Julie and Jack waved to their teammates and walked over to where Sam was parking his car.

'Capt. Reynolds and Lt. Barker want to

see the two of you right away,' Julie told them, 'and we have a new report for them and for you.'

'We'll get the lieutenant on our way to the captain's office,' Sam replied. 'That way everyone can be brought up to date at once.'

Five minutes later, the four detectives and Lt. Baker were sitting in the captain's large office explaining the events of the last several days.

'The facility's records of the suspect, from what we've been told,' Jamie was saying, 'would appear to be the exact opposite of the man we know as 'Blue Man'.'

'The owner/waitress of the diner we stopped at twice in Needles told us a horror story about the facility from her unwanted stay after she had a supposed mental breakdown in Yuma,' Sam added, 'which isn't far from Sunnydale.'

'This happened about thirty years ago,' Jamie continued. 'At that time, shock therapy was still being used routinely in some establishments. However, our subject indicated that mind and mood altering drugs were also given as a matter of course and in large doses. The lawyers were unable to establish the validity of these claims and advised their clients to accept a settlement that would reimburse them for the lawyers' fees, continued payments for a therapist of their choice over the next three years and allow money for the parents to retire, leaving the subject in control of the diner after her therapy ended.'

'The records of the settlement,' Sam informed the group, 'were supposedly sealed under a court order. According to our witness, no gag order was made, but without the court records, everything is hearsay and unprovable after all of this time.'

'So you think that 'Blue Man' has had his personality altered?' Capt. Reynolds questioned.

'From what the waitress told us about her experiences,' Jamie told him, 'and if the facility hasn't altered their methods, I believe that Jonah could very probably have been made criminally insane. Of course, that would have to be determined by a licensed, and court ordered, mental health professional who was not in any way associated with the Sunnydale Psychiatric Board and Care Facility since that is outside of my expertise.'

'From what happened to Mr. Monroe earlier today,' Julie reported to the group, 'we think that something may have been done to the person believed to be Jonah Wilson, AKA 'Blue Man'.'

Sam frowned as he said, 'You told us outside that you and Jack had some news to tell us. Perhaps now would be a good time to make your report.'

Julie took out her notebook from her jacket pocket and opened it. She referred to her notes as she told them everything that had happened at the hospital. 'Because the IV bag, in which a keen eyed, quick thinking nurse had spotted a needle prick near the top, has been placed in the hazmat incinerator, and due to the strength of the anti-toxins used, the doctor felt that it would be highly unlikely to determine the type and strength of the poison used.'

'The doctor did say,' Jack took up the

report, 'that the symptoms were indicative of a strong, fast acting compound that caused paralysis in the lungs and diaphragm, thereby causing respiratory distress. He also concluded that, even with the anti-toxin, if the IV bag had not been removed, the patient would have died from his inability to breathe.'

'I'll see if I can find a judge to issue a subpoena of Mr. Wilson's medical and psychiatric history,' Capt. Reynolds told them as he wrote a memo to himself. 'Good work, everyone. Now, let's find this person before someone else is injured or killed.' With that, he dismissed everyone from his office.

10

'I've got to get hold of that journal Mrs. Smythe-Jones' family kept,' Jonah Wilson mused to himself, as he reviewed the books he had stolen. Those books revealed the history, and size, of the water table under the dry surface of the lakebed, but not the families that benefited from their ancestors' foreknowledge or those who bought up large tracts of land from desperate and unsuspecting people.

Wilson's obsession with the treatment of those like his ancestors, who were easily deceived or who were forced by threat of harm to themselves, their families, or their property to leave what they had worked hard to build, had become unendurable during the last weeks before he escaped from the facility. He didn't understand the procedures that were being used there, but he did know that he *had* to find, and expose, the truth behind what had happened to dozens of homesteading fanners and potential businessmen and their families over a hundred and twenty years ago. The courts had sided with the usurpers while the victims went broke and became broken men and women. Like his ancestors, their voices cried out in his head for justice.

'The voices of the past,' he vowed aloud, '*will* be heard! Their descendants will be given their rightful due and my great-great-grandfather will finally rest in peace!'

★ ★ ★

Late that night, as the Smythe-Jones household was deep in slumber, a stealthy figure dressed in military surplus store urban, night-time camouflage fatigues and night vision goggles approached the rear entrance of the stately home.

Removing a long, flat tool hidden by his clothing, the intruder began to wedge it between the door's locking mechanism and the frame. He knew that he would have only seconds to disarm the home security alarm. The keypad was within easy access from his point of ingress. He also had the means, with the help of a large deposit to the account of a workman who had installed and set the code for the alarm, to accomplish his intended silent and uninterrupted run of the house.

In a small, glass-door cabinet, he found what he was searching for. The doors had no locks or other security measures. They were held closed by magnetic catches that opened quietly at the press of a finger.

Reaching in, he took out a thick leather and cloth bound journal and placed it in a pouch that he had brought along for that purpose.

As the thief reached the back door, a voice called out, 'Who's there?' The thief quickly stepped through the door into the night and blended in with his surroundings to wait for whoever might follow him.

Samantha quickly went to the nearby wall phone and dialed the emergency number. When the operator came on, Samantha told her story of the presumed break-in. Though she was nervous and had to be prompted for information, she was able to give a precise account of her short encounter. She was instructed to stay on the line while waiting for the uniformed patrol officers to arrive and to allow none of the other household members to go outside.

'You're sure that the intruder is not still in the house?' the operator asked, seeking to keep Samantha calm.

'I heard the back door close,' she reported as Mr. Smythe-Jones cautiously turned on various lights on the ground floor. 'The master has switched on some lights and there appears to be no one here but the family.'

There was a knocking at the front door and a powerful Mag-Lite flashlight was being shone in the back area of the property.

The sound of someone climbing over the wall between the deputy mayor's house and the neighbor's behind it, the shout of 'Police! Freeze!' and the sound of running feet through the back yard could be heard.

The police officer at the front door

quickly ran to the aid of her partner as she heard the noise from the back. The other officer was on his radio-phone to the dispatcher giving a quick report of what he had seen and heard.

After making his report, Corporal Stevens informed his partner, 'The suspect climbed over the wall, Janice. He's loose somewhere in the neighborhood. Dispatch has put out a BOLO on him.'

The officers went back to the now open back door and went inside to interview the intended victims.

Janice questioned the housekeeper while Officer Stevens interviewed the other members of the household.

'Do you know what the thief may have been after?' Janice asked.

Samantha looked around, and then spied the space in the small cabinet.

'The family journal of the missus is gone,' she cried. 'It's been in the family for generations! Why would someone want to steal a family heirloom?'

'The Library Thief has taken an interesting collection of historical records over the last several days,' Stevens answered from the other side of the room. 'I think that 'Blue Man' may have wanted it to accomplish his idea of justice for what happened a long time ago.'

'I'll let dispatch know that the perp may have been Lt. Holmes' mystery man,' Janice said, reaching for her hand-held radio.

'Are you telling me that the man who invaded my home,' Mr. Smythe-Jones said in shocked disbelief, 'could have been the same man who probably caused the death of my son?'

No easy, or pat, answers were forthcoming and no words of comfort could be given, so Janice Reid and Joe Stevens closed their notebooks and waited for the arrival of the investigative detectives.

★   ★   ★

'This case seems to keep coming back to the Smythe-Jones family,' Jack observed. 'Why has our man fixated on them? It can't just be all coincidence.'

'More like he has a list of certain important families from the early homestead days,' Sam replied. 'According to my maternal grandmother's journal, when her grandparents immigrated to America, there was a growing colony of British expatriates who were homesteading or buying land on and around an old dry lakebed several miles east of the Santa Ana River. They staked a small claim with a fair potential of profitability once the proposed irrigation canal project was completed. The underground water table was discovered before the project was much more than a trench. Those who could afford to have irrigation wells drilled began to make money from the crops that could be grown in the soil. Feed crops for cattle and other livestock were the next money makers. Others began investing in shops and other businesses that supported the farms and ranches. By the early twentieth century, light industry and military stations added to the growth of London.'

'So,' Jamie commented, 'those who didn't stay lost out on the benefits of a growing economy?'

'That's right, Jamie,' Sam nodded. 'Some of the people who failed to wisely make use of the opportunities available to them in the places that they moved to felt cheated and filed suit. The courts found against them.'

Sam continued his history lesson of London, California, and of both sides of his family.

'And your house was part of the original homestead?' Julie asked.

'That's right,' Sam answered. 'Sherlock had the bee farm in England and his wife had inherited land both in Northern California and next door to the Holmes' property. My maternal great-great-grand-parents settled here in London.'

As the discussion continued, Julie began to get a feel for the thefts and homicides, both successful and attempted. She decided to voice her thoughts when the team met the next morning.

'I am beginning to think that our suspect has developed an 'idee fixe' about what happened so long ago. If I'm right, Sam, you could end up on his enemies list.'

'Jamie and I have also considered that,' Sam responded, 'and we have taken steps that are not, we hope, obvious to Wilson.

146

We would prefer to take him into custody and have him examined by a source known and trusted by us. I believe his true state of mind is essential to ending what may be an ongoing process of at least four generations.'

'You're thinking that the Sunnydale people may have their own agenda?' Jack's face became a study in puzzlement. 'What have they done? Created a version of the 'Manchurian Candidate'?'

'I can't be certain,' Jamie replied, 'but your supposition could be more right than we know.'

'Janice's story,' Sam continued, 'and what we can surmise from Jonah Wilson's alleged activities, along with Sunnydale's closed mouthed reactions, give us plenty of reasons to be extremely cautious at this point in our investigations.'

★   ★   ★

'I had no idea,' Jack remarked to Julie after the meeting, 'that Sam's extended family was so well connected. Did you?'

'Only some,' Julie answered. 'Jamie and

I talked a little and she told me that she and Sam were direct descendants of the original Holmes and Watson. Their adventures and cases were published as fiction, mostly in the *Strand* and *Collier's* magazines before being sold in hardback.'

'And we've been assigned to work with this illustrious team?'

'As the old bromide says, 'make hay while the sun shines'!'

Jack and Julie worked, each wrapped in their own thoughts. Neither would be prepared for later events.

★   ★   ★

Janey and her day shift waitress were just straightening the diner after the breakfast rush when three men dressed in expensively tailored suits walked in. The largest and most unfriendly of the three held up his hand like a traffic officer as Janey approached to greet them.

'Where's the proprietor of this eating establishment?' His voice was deep and raspy.

'You're looking at her,' Janey replied.

'Have a seat anywhere you like. There're plenty of tables available.'

The speaker grabbed her by the hair and twisted her around after a second man backhanded her across the face. The third man pulled a large caliber automatic pistol from a shoulder holster that had been hidden by his suit coat and told the waitress and the cook to stay where they were and no one would get hurt.

'We just want to have a little chat with your boss,' he explained.

'Now, Missy,' the first man said calmly, as if he were ordering a meal from a menu as he twisted her hair even tighter in his fist. The second man moved behind and had pulled her arms up in a painfully high position behind her back that made her cry out in agony. 'We have a message for you from your past: keep your mouth shut, or back you go to where you hoped you'd never be again.'

With that, the three men turned and walked out, leaving an angry Janey and her two frightened employees.

'They're not going to do this to me again!' Janey vowed as she went to her office and began searching for the business cards that the two detectives from London had left with her. 'This time they're gonna be shut down!'

While Janey was making the call to the LPD Robbery-Homicide Division's direct line, the cook went next door to the filling station and used the phone there to call the Needles police and report the incident. The uniformed officers and detectives arrived in record time and began taking individual notes from all three witnesses.

'Considering the upsetting circumstances,' the senior detective told them when the interviews were completed, 'you have all done remarkably well. We have detailed accounts and descriptions of everything that happened. Ms. Atfield, you said that they made a threat about making you relive, or return to, an event or place in your past. Would you please elaborate?'

Janey briefly summarized her time in Sunnydale, Arizona. When she finished, she also explained about the visit from the two LPD detectives and relayed their interest in the psychiatric facility's activities in the past and present.

'They said that they would leave London first thing in the morning,' she informed the detectives. 'They offered to share what they knew with investigators here. They implied that their case was related to things happening in London, Sunnydale and here.'

'Have them call me,' Detective Hector, the senior detective, said, 'as soon as they arrive tomorrow. The more everyone knows, the quicker these bullies can be corralled.'

'Thank you, Detective,' Janey replied. 'It's been thirty years since events nearly ruined my life, and that of my parents. I thought that I had put everything behind me.'

Detective Hector and his partner put away their notebooks and, with assuring words, left the diner.

'When we get back to headquarters,' Detective Hector told his partner, 'I want you to pull everything you can find related to Ms. Atfield's story. The more we know, the better our questions will be when the LPD detectives arrive.'

'Yes, sir,' the younger man replied. 'I'll get on it right away.'

The two detectives arrived in the division room early the next day and waited for Janey to call and say that Detective Holmes and Dr. Watson were waiting at the diner for them.

About the time that Detectives Hector and Richards were deciding to go to the diner and wait for the visiting detectives from Riverside County, Detective Hector's desk phone rang.

'Crimes against Persons and Property division, Detective Hector speaking,' he answered.

Janey told him that Lt. Samuel Holmes and Jamesina Watson *MD, FME*, had just arrived and were having coffee as they waited.

'We'll be there in ten minutes,' Hector informed her.

Detectives Hector and Richards arrived within the stated time and met with the out of town personnel at a booth toward the back of the diner.

After introductions and handshakes

were made, the foursome began trading information. Sam and Jamie received a detailed account of the harassment perpetrated the day before. When Hector and Richards were finished, Sam and Jamie related the events that had been happening in London and the tentative conclusions that their team had reached.

'Ms. Atfield did mention that this case may have begun some thirty years ago,' Richards agreed. 'I've researched everything I could find related to what she told us. Of course, the details were confidential and some of the records were under court ordered seal. Most of what we have is willing testimony from the plaintiff and corroborated by what little there is of recorded events.'

'The defendants that are still available,' Sam revealed, 'are not willing to part with a lot of helpful and historical information. I think that they are trying to cover up past indiscretions and do not welcome any intrusive investigations.'

'Janey's testimony is based on very painful and half buried memories,' Jamie added. 'The actions taken by our suspect

153

in London are highly suspicious and have had dangerous repercussions to several of our citizens.'

'You make it sound as if your suspect has been programmed in some way,' Hector commented.

'I only have a basic knowledge of psychology,' Jamie replied, 'but everything does point to him being controlled somehow.'

'No one can predict the actions of another,' Sam added, 'however; one's past actions can indicate one's future actions. That's what makes our job doable.'

After a long morning discussing every detail that either set of detectives knew, it was agreed that Sam and Detective Bernard Hector would arrange another meeting with Dr. Kindle. The appointment was made for early the next morning.

11

'I don't like it!' the officious man fumed. 'All of these questions from so many different officials. The only group not involved yet is the Psychiatric Board of Review. Our Jonah has got to be shut down. By any means available!

The large man with the cold eyes and demeanor nodded and quietly left to gather his cohorts and prepare for travel.

'If anyone can fix this problem,' the man behind the desk mused under his breath, 'Goliath and his team can.'

⋆　⋆　⋆

Goliath sneered as walked with his cohorts to the Cadillac hybrid in the parking lot and said, 'These eggheads will do just about anything to keep their little secrets under wraps. 'By any means available' he says. What that means is we do what needs doin' but we don't let him know a thing.'

155

'Plausible deniability,' Short Sam observed. 'That's what they call it nowadays.'

'Long as we don't get caught,' Jake added, 'and nothing leads back to our principle, we are home free. I like it.'

The threesome grinned at each other as they got into the car and drove away.

★ ★ ★

'Our suspect keeps avoiding capture,' Jack complained. 'It's as if he were leading a charmed life!'

'It appears as if someone is hiding in the shadows,' Julie replied, 'and when Jonah looks like he's in trouble, this person pulls some strings, and, 'poof', our man disappears.

'I don't like the way he just 'happened' to elude his keeper in Arizona shortly before he showed up at the Victorian Reading Room. Where did he get his traveling money and who told him what books he needed? How did he know where to find them?'

'Yeah, it's a real puzzler,' Jack groused. 'Someone certainly knows more than they're letting on.'

★　★　★

'Detectives Holmes and Hector have arrived, Dr. Kindle,' Sandra, his secretary, said over the phone intercom.

'Alright,' Dr. Kindle told her. 'Send them in.'

The two detectives entered and were invited to sit down in the plush client chairs opposite Dr. Kindle.

'And what can I do for you today, detectives?' Kindle asked as he leaned back in his ergonomic office chair. 'Have you found our missing patient?'

'Not yet,' Sam answered. 'However, we do have some questions about an incident involving one of your former patients.'

'Detective Holmes.' Kindle gave Sam an exasperated stare. 'You know that, ethically, I cannot talk about our patients' case histories. Current or former.'

'This, as far as we know, doesn't directly involve the personal history of our victim or her time here. A threat was made saying that her past would be a lot better than what would happen if she were to reveal certain things about her breakdown.'

'In other words, you are claiming imminent danger?'

'According to her statement,' Detective Hector replied, 'that is our belief and the reason for our asking for your help in understanding where the possible danger may be coming from.'

'I understand, Detective,' Kindle offered, 'however, there is not a whole lot that I can tell you. Not even under these circumstances.'

'Perhaps the court records can be unsealed,' Sam reflected, 'and she can give us a better account of the events of thirty years ago.'

'That would be your prerogative,' Kindle said a little nervously, 'but I don't see how it would help you.'

'It would allow her to legally speak freely about the time she spent under your facility's care.'

'And it would give you complete freedom for rebuttal to any of her allegations,' Hector added.

'I'll have to speak with our attorneys before I say anything else, gentlemen.' Kindle stood up and offered his hand in dismissal. 'Please feel free to contact me after, and if you obtain a release of the court documents.'

The detectives were shown out and the door was apparently closed upon their line of inquiry.

'Did he seem a little worried about what Ms. Atfield might reveal?' Hector asked Sam as they got into the car.

Sam thought about the interview, and then said, 'I think that there is a lot going on that we may never fully understand.'

'Like, maybe why the records of her lawsuit were sealed,' Hector reflected, 'and why a gag order was issued?'

'It does seem like an unlikely ruling, doesn't it?'

The two men drove away, unsatisfied after their time with the director of the Sunnydale Psychiatric Board and Care Facility.

12

Goliath and his team had arrived in London very late in the afternoon. Referring to the information that they had from their patron, they went to the rented apartment where Jonah Wilson was last known be residing.

Using their knowledge of illegal entry techniques, the three men began to look for evidence of their target's presence. The stolen books were found hidden in a concealed compartment in a large luggage case in the hall closet.

'Not very inventive,' Jake remarked at the ease with which they found their prey's hidden stash.

'Simple enough to have been overlooked,' Short Sam responded.

'Of course,' Goliath added with a malicious grin, 'No one else would have had our inside information. Now, all we have to do is to wait for our little chicken to come home to roost.'

The trio settled down outside the apartment complex, waiting for Jonah to return home.

★ ★ ★

As Jonah walked up to the door of his apartment, he sensed that something was amiss. He looked around for the source of his uneasiness, but found nothing.

He had placed his key in his door when he was grabbed from behind by a large, powerful hand holding a cloth that gave off a sweet odor and he quickly lost consciousness.

Sometime later, he awakened feeling lightheaded, with his limbs tightly bound. Before he could utter a sound, a piece of duct tape was slapped across his mouth and a large, dangerous-looking man sat him upright.

'Good to see that you're awake,' the man-mountain said. 'If you're a good boy, we may just return you to where you escaped from and forget about your little jaunt. The boss said to make you go away as a problem, by any means available. You can help us to help you, or you can get seriously hurt. Do you understand me? Nod your head if you do.'

Jonah vigorously nodded his head in answer.

Before he could begin thinking of a way out of his dilemma, he felt a sharp sting and then he felt no more.

'He should be out for several hours,' Jake informed his partners. 'Do we take him back to Sunnydale, or make sure he never wakes up?'

'We quiz the boss about what he wants done with the package of 'damaged goods',' said Goliath after some careful thought. 'If he leaves it up to us, we trash the package as spoilage and head home.'

'And if he wants to inspect the damages?' asked Short Sam.

'If that's the boss' decision, he goes trussed up like a Christmas present,' the large man replied. 'Maybe he'll want to find out what went wrong.'

The three, after a quick check of the streets, earned their prisoner to their vehicle and drove away, Goliath in the passenger seat using his cell.

Unknown to any of the three men, a 'bag lady' of indeterminate age and ethnic background had seen the abduction of the fourth man. She used her cell phone to speed dial a special contact.

'The 'Blue Man' has just been taken from his abode,' she said without preliminaries, when the phone at the other end of the connection was answered. 'Three Caucasian males just put him in the trunk of a gray Cadillac hybrid sedan with Arizona vanity plates saying 'NOFEEBS', headed southeast. Our man was tied up and apparently unconscious.'

'*Vielen dank,*' the answer came as she disconnected.

'What's going on Jack?' Julie asked her partner.

'That was my confidential informant who likes to work undercover as an East German resistance informer,' he informed her. 'She dresses like a bag lady and likes the code names of 'J.R.' and 'Joan Rivermom'. She's been following Jonah Wilson for me. Hoping to find out where he has been staying. Our 'Blue Man' has just been abducted and placed in the trunk of a gray Cadillac hybrid sedan being used by three men.'

Jack continued to fill Julie in on 'J.R.'s information as he drove to the southeast quadrant of the city.

Julie grabbed the mike for the unmarked's radio and relayed instructions for all units in that area to be on look-out for the suspect vehicle.

'Maybe we've caught a break,' she said as she replaced the microphone. 'Sam and Jamie may have knocked over the anthill.'

'Sam is supposed to be in Arizona with a detective from Needles,' Jack reminded her, 'but Jamie was going to stay at the diner in case those three enforcers came back.'

'At least she'll have the other detective from Needles with her for backup,' Julie commented. 'Barritsu against three men with guns is not very good odds.'

Jack went silent as he continued his search for the suspects' vehicle.

★   ★   ★

164

The administrator who resembled the stereotypical psychiatrist entered Dr. Kindle's office. He wore a satisfied look.

'We have a report that our subject will be returned in a few hours,' he reported. 'We should have him under secure confinement by this evening.'

'Any problems in getting him away?' Dr. Kindle asked. 'The LPD will surely want him available for questioning, at the very least.'

'That has all been dealt with.'

13

Jamie closed her phone and said to Detective Richards, 'Our suspect was kidnapped a short while ago. My associates back at the LPD believe that his captors may be taking him back to Sunnydale.'

'Perhaps we should inform Detectives Holmes and Hector before they get too far from the facility?' Richards suggested.

'Sam has already been contacted on his cell phone,' Jamie told him. 'He and Detective Hector turned around, found a motel, and set up a watch for the vehicle said to belong to the kidnappers.'

'Ah, the virtue of efficiency,' Richards sighed.

★　★　★

'Do we stop in Needles on the way back?' Short Sam asked, as they traveled toward the state line.

'No need,' Goliath replied. 'We filled

the gas tank just outside London, so we should be good on fuel until we are well inside Arizona. Nice mileage on these new generation hybrid engines. The large fuel tank on this make of sedan is a plus, too.'

'What about a personal pit stop?' Jake asked.

'That is something you should have taken care of earlier,' he was told derisively. 'Now you'll just have to hold your water until we get to Yuma.'

'Alright,' Jake said from the back seat, 'but don't blame me for the ruined upholstery!'

Both Goliath and Short Sam laughed at Jake's embarrassment.

★　★　★

'According to the time table we have figured,' Hector commented from the lobby of the motel's attached diner, 'our suspects should be passing through any minute.'

'Perhaps they had to make an unscheduled stop somewhere along the way,' Sam shrugged his shoulders. 'One of them could have a small bladder.'

'I hope that is all that is holding them up.'

'Nothing like a long drive to make one appreciate the little comforts in life.'

Just then, a hybrid version of a luxury sedan pulled into the parking lot and an average looking, well-dressed man got out and hurried toward the back area of the diner. The man was in the restroom for several minutes before he came out, looking much relieved.

As he returned to his companions, he said, 'I told you that I didn't think that I'd make all the way it to Yuma. Now maybe you'll listen to me?'

'Yeah, yeah,' the shortest of the three answered with a laugh. 'If you wouldn't drink a whole pot of coffee before taking a long drive, perhaps you would have made it all of the way home!'

'No more arguing, guys,' the biggest man ordered. 'We're running late enough as it is. The boss said that we had just so much time to get back with the goods. The product inspectors are breathing down his neck and the sponsor is getting impatient.'

The three men left quickly and the detectives walked rapidly, but without rushing, to their car and headed in the same direction as their quarry.

'There's no hurry,' Detective Hector said as he got in the car. 'We have a good idea where they will go now.'

'I wouldn't want to guess wrong,' Sam answered, 'not when a man's life may be on the line. Keep them in sight just in case we're mistaken.'

The Cadillac hybrid sedan went almost exactly to where it was expected to go. It came to a windowless brick and stone building at the edge of the facility grounds and parked inside a concealed garage.

'Jonah must be in the trunk,' Sam said as he and Hector watched from an enclosed entryway nearby.

The two taller men opened the trunk and took out a heavy, limp bundle and earned it inside the building.

The short man made a call on his cell phone.

'Dollars to donuts,' Hector commented, 'that's your abductee they just took from that trunk. Do you think he's still alive?'

'From the way they handled their cargo,' Sam replied, 'I'd say that they have drugged their victim.'

★　★　★

The officious man had called the two lead administrators into his office.

'I just received word that our subject has been returned,' he told them. 'Dr. Kindle will check him over physically. You, Dr. Roarshack, will determine if we still have him under our control. We need him mentally pliable and physically healthy.'

'You're certain no one will be looking for him?' Dr. Roarschack asked. 'We don't want a repeat of thirty years ago.'

'My father's mistakes,' the leader told him, 'have been studied and rectified. Wilson has no living relatives and his personal history has been rewritten to fit our needs. Everything has been done right this time.'

'And what about those detectives from

California?' Dr. Kindle questioned, a frown upon his face. 'Their poking into this 'experiment' could get us all arrested and this facility shut down.'

'I've seen to it,' the man stared at the others coldly, 'that their efforts will come to naught before that happens.'

The meeting broke up and each man attended to the chores that awaited him.

★　★　★

'No one will ruin things this time,' the officious man said aloud as soon as he was alone. 'You can come in, Sam.'

Short Sam stepped out of an adjoining alcove to speak to his boss.

'Things went smoothly in London,' he reported. 'Wilson was staying at the place we were told. Goliath expects that he'll be awake within the hour.'

'Good. I'll want to reinforce all of the protocols before he's seen by Drs. Kindle and Roarschack. See that everything will be ready when he awakens.'

'Yes, sir.'

Short Sam executed a perfect military

'about face' and returned to the window-less building to deliver his boss' orders.

★   ★   ★

As Sam and Hector waited for Short Sam to return, they accessed their partners in Needles. They were informed that none of the three tough men had returned and that a fully authorized search of Wilson's apartment had found the missing volumes.

'Julie said that Jack's CI had seen three men go into the building several minutes before Wilson had come home,' Jamie said. 'The apartment was neat, but had definitely been lived in for a while. The building Super told Jack that Wilson had been there for more than a month, but less than two. Also, Wilson had paid cash in advance for a three month stay.'

'I think that the three abductors may have been the ones who paid Janey her visit,' Sam added. 'Detective Hector and I followed them back to a building on the facility's property. We're waiting to see how events here unfold. We'll contact you if we learn anything new.'

'We'll do the same here,' Jamie replied. 'Is there anything else that you need for Jack and Julie to do back in London, or that Detective Hector wants to tell his partner?'

'Just make sure that Ms. Atfield and her people are protected,' Hector said into the phone set on speaker.

★ ★ ★

The officious man was the silent partner and leader of the Sunnydale Psychiatric Board and Care Facility. His father had been one of the three co-founders; Roarschack, Kindle, and Johnstein.

The senior Johnstein had retired rather than allow certain secret efforts of mental and physical control to come to light. The notes on the methods were secretly passed to his son during the debacle with the Atfield family.

'I was on the brink of a profound discovery,' he told his heir, 'when the subject's parents had arrived and removed her from our custody. If the authorities had found out what I was really doing, everyone at the facility would have been held complicit and ruined. The facility would have been closed and our patients removed to more conventional hospitals.'

The junior Johnstein had taken the notes and conclusions and studied them for years before discreetly applying them to new and 'hopelessly insane' subjects.

When Jonah Wilson was admitted, Johnstein felt that he had, at last, found the perfect subject for his new direction of experimental drugs and unconventional therapies.

'He was the perfect blend of neuroses and psychoses to test both my father's and my own theories,' he told himself. 'And he has no living family to interfere. His past can be molded so that it will fit perfectly into whatever we need it to be.'

When Johnstein felt that his experiment was ready for the final test, it was arranged for Wilson to escape. The deeply imposed history would set him upon a predetermined course of action. After a given time of carefully monitored freedom of action, Wilson would be brought back to Sunnydale and re-evaluated.

The experiment had revealed several flaws in controlling the subject. Wilson's determination to complete his impressed goals proved to be stronger than anticipated. Rather than be stopped, or interfered with, he resorted to violent means. He was no longer predictable.

'The drugs must be stronger,' he told his special workers, 'and the special therapies more intense.'

One of the physicians told him, 'The drug levels are dangerously high. Much higher and they could become lethal!'

'Push him,' Johnstein ordered. 'Find the limits of his tolerances, even if our subject dies.'

Now that Wilson was back under control, he would be made into a catatonic lump if it was necessary; to keep him from being examined by someone capable of finding out exactly what types of treatments had been used on him.

★　★　★

Detectives Holmes and Hector saw the officious, late-middle-aged man approach the windowless building, carrying an old-fashioned medical bag in his hand. He looked carefully around the area before entering.

'Do you think he saw us?' Hector asked. 'I think he may be the leader of these men.'

'No, he couldn't have seen us,' Sam answered, 'and I agree that he may have much to reveal, *if* he can be made to tell us. First, we have to find out what is going on inside that building. What could be so useful in that bag? I'm sure that Dr. Watson would have an educated guess if she were here.'

The two detectives silently emerged from their place of concealment. As they approached their goal, they kept a lookout for a way to sneak into the building.

They found a door that was made flat with the south side of the structure. The door had no apparent latch or handle. A gentle push caused the door to swing to the inside.

'If that door is alarmed,' Sam whispered, 'it's too late to do anything about it now. We either go in, hoping to not be discovered, or we run and hope we can get away.'

'We've come too far to back down now,' Hector replied. 'I say we take our chances inside.'

Sam was already stepping through the opening.

'Nice to know that we agree,' Hector sighed as he followed Sam.

The lights inside were set at a restful level and soothing music, played just above a subliminal level, came from hidden speakers.

'Someone intends to soothe the savage beast,' Hector whispered. 'A relaxing environment to give them even more control over their patients.'

'More like subjects,' Sam replied. 'I think these people are attempting some form of mental and physical control experiment. That would fit in with Wilson's change in behavior pattern and with what Ms. Atfield experienced during her stay here.'

'That theory seems too bizarre to be true!'

'Bizarre enough for a thirty-year cover-up.'

The two detectives searched the building for any sign of the occupants they knew had to be present and for evidence of questionable activities.

Locked doors barred their entrance into several rooms before they found a room with a light coming through the slightly ajar opening.

Sam took the left side of the door as Hector took the right. Faint moans could be heard from their position in the hallway, but nothing else.

Hector was nearest the barely-open entryway, so he pressed his eye to the crack and peeked inside. In his limited view, he saw what appeared to be a hospital bed with restraints holding a figure in place.

'There seems to be someone restrained in there,' he vocalized, almost inaudibly. 'Do we check inside, or do we go for backup?'

Sam gestured his desire to go inside and held up three fingers as he began a silent countdown. When the final finger was closed, Hector pushed the door open, his service revolver in his hand. Sam followed, shoving the door backward to make sure that they weren't attacked from behind.

Once inside, they found a person strapped to the bed, eyes wild with pain, slack mouth drooling.

'I don't know who she is,' Sam said in dismay. 'I'll get some shots of the scene here, and then let's go before we're caught.'

Hector kept a lookout until Sam was done. Then they both worked their way back to the door where they had come in. They were almost at their goal when they heard two male voices in the hall they had just left.

'The patient in 4B is due for her next round of treatments,' a voice that they had heard at the motel diner said. 'She'll be ready for the boss by tomorrow morning.'

The two men turned into the room the detectives had recently vacated.

The detectives did not wait any longer to make their exit and quickly work their way to their concealed vehicle. Once they were in the car, they made themselves scarce and hoped that they had not been discovered.

★   ★   ★

'I've got a friend in the FBI who would love to have a piece of this,' Hector told Sam. 'Do you think we have enough evidence that federal laws have been broken so that we can bring him in?'

'We could probably make a case for kidnapping and transportation across state lines,' replied Sam. 'But it looks weak right now.'

They had been driving for some time without any sign of having been followed. They were now less than fifteen minutes from Janey's diner.

'I'm going to check in with Janey and our partners,' Sam said. 'Maybe Dr. Watson has some news from London.'

Sam opened his cell phone and speed-dialed Jamie. He was about to disconnect when Jamie answered.

'Sam?' she answered breathlessly. 'Are

180

you and Detective Hector on your way back? Are you both okay?'

'Bernard and I are about ten minutes away.' He noted the concern in his partner's voice as he asked, 'What's happened while we were gone?'

'This morning, PI Monroe was released from the hospital in London,' she reported. 'Fifteen minutes after he picked up his car from the evidence yard, he stopped at an AM/PM filling station and convenience store to buy gas and a large coffee. As he pulled away from the pump, his vehicle exploded. The attendant quickly used the emergency switch to shut down the pumps, but not before the one that Monroe had used caught fire. Emergency responders rapidly arrived and put out the fire. Monroe and his car were both a total loss.'

'Any ideas about what caused the explosion?' Sam inquired. 'Fifteen minutes seems a long time between the first start and the big boom.'

'Forensics is still collecting the pieces,' Jamie said. 'Julie and Jack talked to one of the people on site who said that Monroe had just placed the nozzle back on the pump, started his vehicle, and was pulling away when it disintegrated in a ball of flame, smoke and noise.'

'Perhaps the bomb was remote controlled,' Sam remarked thoughtfully. 'The big question is how, when and where the bomb was installed, and why the investigators didn't discover it. You and I were out in the parking lot at Johanna's within minutes of the attack on Monroe.'

'We've theorized that Wilson was the perp for the attack,' Jamie said, 'but what if the bomb was planted during the attack? We've always wondered before how 'Blue Man' always seemed to vanish after his crimes. Either he was extremely lucky, or he has had a guardian angel watching over him.'

'I think Jack may need more details from his CI,' Sam decided. 'Wilson's kidnapping was a little too easy.'

Sam almost disconnected when he remembered the photos he had taken. 'I'm sending you some photos from my phone. E-mail them to Jack and Julie. If the person in them can be identified, I want to know. They were taken inside a

blockhouse type of building on the facility's property. Bernard and I saw three
men take a man-sized bundle wrapped in
a quilt or a blanket inside. It may have
been Wilson in a dragged state.'

'I'll send Julie and Jack the pictures as
soon as I get them. If they need enhanc-
ing, Julie knows someone she can go to.'

Jamie set up her phone to place the
pictures into an encrypted attachment in
her laptop's e-mail. She quickly wrote an
explanation for Julie and sent them.

14

'You're sure that Monroe died in the explosion?' Johnstein asked the person on the phone. 'No more bungling?'

When the answer was given in the positive, he added, 'I've got another job for you. You'll use Goliath and his team this time.'

Johnstein took several minutes giving explicit instructions and then disconnected.

'Goliath,' he said as he turned to his chief lieutenant. 'I want Jackstone's assignment to succeed, but I don't want him to survive and leave evidence of his having been the one who planted and detonated the bomb on Monroe's car left where it will be found after a reasonably difficult search is made. Nothing is to lead law enforcement officials back here. Understood?'

'Understood, Boss.'

Goliath gathered his men to go meet the doomed Jackstone.

* ★ ★

'This case just keeps getting uglier and more complicated,' Detective Jack Roberts commented, with a look of puzzled frustration on his face. 'Somebody is working overtime to make sure he stays in the wings and out of sight.'

'This whole set of related incidents is nothing but a big FUBAR,' Sgt. Julie Simon remarked thoughtfully, as she reread the e-mail and took another look at the pictures that Dr. Jamesina Watson had sent. 'Every time we think we know where this case is headed, the stage director changes the scene.'

'I wonder if our main perp isn't just winging it,' Jack added. 'All of the circumstantial evidence points to the Sunnydale facility, but the smoking gun is still missing.'

'Let's go back to the conference room Sam set up and review the known facts,' Julie suggested, 'and see if we can begin to develop a reasonable theory.'

In the conference room, Julie added copies of the photographs received in

Jamie's email to the cork board. From her notes, she added any new information as she updated the white board.

Jack also worked on the updates, eliminating theories that were no longer viable.

As he looked the boards over, his face lit up with an idea. He took a writing pad and a pencil and began to design a flow chart of the sequence of events since Jonathan Smythe-Jones' death. He carefully placed events that were not known first hand into a 'best guess' chronology with numbers in parentheses indicating the order that they were learned or discovered.

'We are being led to believe,' he said, when he had arranged his chart to his satisfaction, 'that the reasons behind this go back to the founding of London and the discovery of the underground lake.'

'But you think the beginning of this case may have started sooner than that?' Julie looked at Jack quizzically. 'How much sooner? And where?'

'The 'where' is out in Arizona,' Jack said, 'and probably at the facility. 'When' could have begun with Janey Atfield's unwanted stay there. Jonah Wilson has also spent time there. It's the best connection that I can see right now.'

'Let's sift through this some more,' Julie responded. 'We'll set up our new theories and take turns knocking them down. That seems to work for people in the novels, why not for us?'

★   ★   ★

As Julie and Jack worked on theories in London, Sam and Jamie discussed the discoveries made in Sunnydale at a table at Janey's diner. Detectives Hector and Roberts had needed to return to their headquarters, asking to be kept in the loop.

'If only we could get the cooperation from the facility's administrators that we've received from our opposite numbers here in Needles,' Sam remarked in frustration, 'we'd be ready to make an arrest by now.'

'Unfortunately,' Jamie frowned as she sipped her iced tea, 'my medical colleagues have more restrictions when disseminating, and sharing, information than our fellow cops. But if I were in trouble, I'd want the same protections that we are required to give any other citizen.'

'I would, too, Jamie.' Sam then changed the subject's focus. 'I wonder how our partners are doing? The thefts have been solved and the stolen books have been located and are waiting to be returned. Our suspect in Smythe-Jones' death has been kidnapped and hidden away.'

Sam was ready to take out his frustration on the first person that blocked his path. Jamie touched his arm and gently offered to drive them back to London.

'We can take another look at our evidence boards and shake our theories loose and see what falls out,' she said, as Janey stopped at their table.

'You know,' she said as she placed a slice of peach cobbler before each of them. 'When my folks rescued me from that hellhole, I had a huge gap in my memories. The years of therapy brought most of them back, but the nightmares never totally left. Until you two walked in here looking for information on that man who escaped from Sunnydale, I never fully realized what they did to me there. If there is any way to keep others from going through all of that, I'll help any way I'm able. By the way, the cobbler has already been included as part of your original bill.'

* * *

The return trip to London was spent in quiet contemplation as the partners reviewed the events of the last few days. By the time they came within the area where the road signs began to give the distance to London, Jamie was feeling uneasy about their lack of progress. It seemed as if they took three steps back for every step forward. She was about to vocalize her feelings when Sam spoke.

'Great-grandfather would have called this a 'five pipe problem' as he spent the whole evening and into the late morning reviewing clues and evidence.' He heaved a disgusted sigh before continuing. 'There has to be a missing puzzle piece. Perhaps Jack and Julie have the right idea.'

'Their last report said they were taking a closer look at our compiled facts and theories,' Jamie said. 'Perhaps you and I should stand back and take a look at the bigger picture.'

'They're busy looking at the individual trees,' Sam grinned, 'while we should take a look at the entire forest? That does sound like a fair division of labor.'

15

The windowless building was far enough away from the main buildings that the thickness of its sound-proofed walls prevented any noise from inside being heard by the conventional therapists or their patients. Now that Patient Wilson had been returned to Sunnydale, the 'isolation therapy' building contained three occupants. Each patient had no contact with anyone but the faceless 'Doctor Anonymous' who visited twice daily to administer 'treatments' and to ask a repeated series of questions. If the answers were unsatisfactory, the patient was given a painful 'treatment' intended to remind the patient of the proper response.

Johnstein, AKA 'Doctor Anonymous', looked at the awake, but senses-dulled, patient before him.

'You have been a bad boy, Jonah,' he said in a monotone. 'Running away was okay. That was part of the plan. But all of that violence! You weren't supposed to do that yet. We just wanted you to take a few books, take down some notes, and get back here. We've had to retrieve you and clean up the mess you caused. You now have to be given a triple treatment.'

Jonah's body arched and strained against the thick bindings that kept him from falling out of the bed, his mouth shut tight against the scream that tried to escape.

'Fight against it all you want,' the hated voice droned. 'It will do you no good. You will not be allowed to behave in any manner that we don't wish. The sooner you accept your conditioning, the sooner the pain will end.'

After the treatment had run its course and the patient fell into an exhausted sleep, Johnstein had an orderly administer the drug that allowed the patient to be manipulated like a puppet.

'Between the drugs and the treatments,' he spoke into a Dictaphone recorder, 'the subject should become completely docile and trainable. The next outing will be better-controlled and should give us better results. The subject's will has proven to be stronger than we realized. However, I believe that it will soon be fully repressed.'

Johnstein wrote on a notepad, removed the page, and handed it to the orderly who was standing by his side.

'Print out copies of this schedule and give them to the doctors listed.' he said without looking at the man. They are not; repeat *not*, to deviate in any way.'

★ ★ ★

Dr. Kindle looked at his two colleagues and remarked, 'These tests are getting too dangerous. The subjects have already been damaged beyond hope of a return to normalcy.'

'What can we do?' the youngest, a woman whose name was Rachael Bennet, asked. 'After all, Mr. Johnstein and his father have been conducting these experiments for a very long time without adverse effects.'

'What do you call causing great bodily harm, directly or indirectly, stealing valuable property, and Lord knows what else? None of the patients who have been given the complete set of treatments have ever been healthy enough to return to society.'

Dr. Roarschack let out a loud sigh. 'Rachael has a point, Thomas. The Johnsteins originally set up the treatment protocols and now have our careers at their mercy. Even the future of this facility is under their control.'

'Someday that will all come crashing down on all our heads,' Kindle fumed. 'Thirty years ago, this facility was almost shut down and all of our personnel nearly lost their licenses. As it was, this facility had to pay a huge indemnity and a severe loss of prestige that has only now begun to return to what it was before. Something must be done before it's too late.'

★   ★   ★

Rachael Bennet left with her mind confused and her emotions in turmoil. Robbery couldn't be part of her lover's plan. He just wanted a way to change unhealthy behavior so that the mentally disturbed could lead a normal and productive life. She had to warn Joseph about what Drs. Kindle and Roarschack were contemplating.

Rachael hurried to Joseph's office only to find that he was not in. She knew that he had special projects in the bunker building. Perhaps he was there.

Rachael opened the door to the bunker building and began calling Johnstein's name. After frantically opening doors in search of her lover and mentor, she looked in upon a scene that she never would have believed she would see.

'I'm sorry,' she said as she backed out of the door. 'I was just looking for Mr. Johnstein.'

The woman strapped to her bed lay naked and spread-eagled while a man was on top of her in a compromising position.

'Too bad that you came in just now,' a familiar voice said behind her. 'I can't let you leave here now.'

A hand covered her mouth before she could scream and she felt the prick of a hypodermic needle in her neck.

'Too bad about your undiscovered

heart condition, my dear,' Johnstein said as Rachael collapsed in his arms.

★ ★ ★

Jackstone met Goliath and company in front of the restaurant.

'All set to go?' he asked the big man. 'It's a long drive to London.'

'Everything has been packed in the car,' Goliath nodded. 'You get in the back with Jake and we'll be off. Oh, better take care of everything before we leave. We won't be making any pit stops along the way. You too, Jake.'

With a scowl on his face, Jake followed Jackstone into the restaurant's men's room.

'Maybe we should lose Jake on this assignment, too,' Short Sam commented dryly.

'And maybe I'll be the one to make it back,' Goliath muttered under his breath.

Jackstone and Jake returned and the four men headed to the freeway.

'I don't like cops,' Jackstone complained, 'but whacking them always brings more trouble than it's worth.'

'The boss says it has to be done,' said Goliath from the front seat as he drove. 'These two got a reputation for putting people away. Some of them, permanently. The trash gets taken out and that's that.'

★ ★ ★

'So, this is where we are with our revised theories,' Julie said, as she finished her presentation. 'Everything we know, or believe we know, has been distilled until we have removed all of the imperfections out of our logic. Any comments?'

'Eliminating the impossible,' Sam spoke up, 'is the first step in discovering the truth. Now we begin sorting the improbable into its component parts so that we can find a theory that fits the facts.'

'I think that someone has been purposely playing with people's minds,' Jamie reflected, almost to herself. 'How else do we explain Wilson's behavior and the events surrounding him? Nothing makes sense unless this is true.'

'So,' Jack asked, 'who is the puppet

197

master and how do we flush him out?'

'I think we may have begun to upset his applecart, so to speak,' Sam replied. 'Our actions have made the suspected controller's plans become somewhat unraveled. If we can just keep pushing the right buttons, he may do something that will give himself away. Everyone needs to be extra sensitive to their surroundings now. Our quarry is getting nervous. Lt. Baker needs to be apprised of our concerns.'

Sam gathered up his notes from the meeting and walked to Baker's office. Getting permission to enter, Sam laid out the team's theories and concerns, before suggesting a plan to bring about the capture and legal ending of this warped intelligence.

'I'll get the authorizations from the Arizona State authorities for the arrests and extraditions,' Baker said 'We need to have this done by the book. No one gets a 'get out of jail free' card because of an un-dotted 'I' or an uncrossed 'T'.'

Sam returned to his team and they began to set their plans into motion.

Goliath and his team arrived in London after dark and took rooms in an economy motel.

'We get some rest,' Goliath told them, 'and then we look for the best way to accomplish our mission and get away. None of the targets are to be left standing.'

The three other men just looked at each other as they put away their luggage. Afterwards, they went to the eatery across the street and took care of their physical needs.

'According to the boss' instructions,' Jackstone commented as they returned to the motel, 'there is to be nothing that leads back to the facility in Arizona. That means that not only do we act quickly, but all of the brass gets picked up and the weapons get sanitized. Any bodies or collaterals that don't belong to the targets get taken to the desert and disposed of discreetly and completely.'

There were nods of understanding all around.

'How soon after we get the warrants and authorizations do you want to serve them?' Jack asked Sam.

'Just as soon as the Arizona state police can get their personnel in place,' Sam answered. 'The more time that it takes to get everyone in place, the more likely that we'll lose the initiative. Timing will be crucial once we start the ball rolling.'

'Rules of Engagement?' Julie wanted to know.

'No one fires a weapon unless fired upon,' Sam replied. 'Those are our orders from the Commissioner. We are working outside of our jurisdiction and we want no questions asked from a defense attorney that would get the whole case thrown out of court.'

'I hope that the Arizona law enforcement is on the same frequency,' Jamie added.

'The Chief and the Captain are working closely with the Sunnydale police force,' Sam told everyone. 'The four of us will meet at headquarters and leave for Sunnydale at dawn tomorrow.'

Everyone put their notes away in their folders and headed out to relax and get some rest for the next day's activities.

Sam and Jamie decided to have a late supper at Johanna's before heading to their separate homes. Johanna greeted them warmly and took them to their usual table.

'The two of you have been out of town a lot lately,' Johanna commented as her guests took their seats. 'I hear that there's been a lot of excitement concerning the library thefts.'

'Well,' Jamie said reluctantly, 'we have gotten the stolen volumes back, but the suspect seems to have been kidnapped and spirited away before we could make an arrest.'

Johanna looked at her, but kept silent.

'We're pretty sure where he was taken,' Sam offered, 'but we don't know why. Everything seems to center upon a mental board and care in Arizona. This case may go back decades.'

'Okay,' Johanna said. 'Since you were out of town when it happened, I won't ask any questions about that PI that got blown up.'

Johanna got up to circulate among her other patrons.

'I see that Johanna still has the repair donation jar on the counter along with the tip jar,' Jamie reflected.

'Yeah,' Sam said. 'I haven't heard anything lately about damages to the restaurant. I guess even the bad guys like to eat and relax here and don't want any trouble with Johanna or her employees.'

'She seems to be a one woman crime prevention detail, all right.'

'At least this place seems to have become the Switzerland of London.'

A familiar face walked through the door. The individual looked around room and, seeing Sam and Jamie, walked over to their table and sat down.

'What happened with the Pulitzer Prize, Rumplestiltskin?' Jamie smiled mischievously. 'Oh that's right, it's Ronald Roberts, isn't it?'

'I missed out by one vote!' was his sad reply. 'But at least the *Midnight Confessor* allowed me to have my old job back. Mister Simon really wants the low down on the murder at the Victorian Reading

Room. It seems that not even the *LonCal Times* has a handle the situation. Can I get an exclusive for old time's sake?'

'Only after the case has been solved, R.R.,' Sam informed him. 'You know the department's rules.'

'I don't even get a hint right now? How many times have I got to be nearly killed to be given special privileges?'

'As many times as it takes to get it right,' a voice said from behind R.R.

'Say hello to our new team partners,' Jamie said. 'Julie, Jack, say hello to the almost Pulitzer Prize winner. R.R., Julie likes my idea of playing 'This Little Piggy' even more than I do.'

'I'm pierced through the heart, Jamie,' R.R. pantomimed. 'All the pretty ladies seem to have it in for me!'

'What has your sleazy tabloid been saying about the Smythe-Jones death, R.R.?' Julie inquired with a sneer. 'Nothing good, I'll bet.'

'Only what the city's finest will allow them to say, my dear.'

'You mean that they no longer make up a story when they can't get information?'

Jack chimed in. 'That's a first.'

'Hey,' R.R. said defensively, 'we're a first rate newspaper, not a yellow journal!'

'Does your friend, Johnny Oh, hear anything?' Sam asked. 'Or any word from that guy in the fancy wheel chair with long ears?'

Jack and Julie looked at each other quizzically. They knew nothing about the two people that Sam referred to.

'Johnny has been out of town for a while,' R.R. answered. 'And our friend in high places hasn't been heard from since the Super-TASER case. Not that I'm anxious for his involvement. The last time I was almost turned into roadkill.'

'We're about to follow some leads that will have to remain our own for now,' Sam said, a finger placed across his lips, 'and nothing else can be said until the case is solved. Of course, if you or your contacts learn anything helpful, we'll allow you the exclusive on the story when it's all over.'

R.R. got up from the table and started for the door. 'Thanks for nothin'. And after all that I've done for you, too.'

When R.R. had gone out of the grill and bar, Julie asked, 'What was all of that about? Who are Johnny Oh and the mysterious man in the wheel chair?'

'Johnny Oh is an information broker that R.R. sometimes gets his leads from and the other man is a deep black ops person whose information helped save the lives of some people very important to me,' Jamie explained. 'The information in both cases was extremely timely.'

16

The following morning, Sam, Jamie, Julie, and Jack met at the department's motor pool and signed out an SUV for their trip to Sunnydale.

'We want to stop in Needles for breakfast and to check up on a person who has given us some very helpful information,' Sam said, just as his cell phone began demanding his attention.

'This may be important,' he told the others as he answered, 'Lt. Holmes. This had better be good.'

'I think that four suspicious men are headed your way,' the voice said. 'Could be bad unless you don't care to get yourselves killed, or worse.'

'Where are they coming from, R.R.?' Sam inquired.

'They're headed north on Central Boulevard just south of King Edward Avenue,' was the reply. 'They seem to be in an awful hurry.'

'Thanks, R.R.,' Sam said. 'That exclusive is yours when this case is over. This current incident is yours to report now if you can get here in time.'

Sam disconnected and told the others what was happening. 'Get the front desk to get us some heavy duty back up, Jamie,' he ordered. 'Julie, Jack, take cover and prepare to return fire. Defend yourselves, but if you can, I want at least one of them alive to answer questions.'

The luxury sedan only took twenty-five seconds to travel the four blocks to the police station. As the vehicle roared up to the parking lot, assault weapons began to open fire from the three passenger windows. Sam and his team returned fire as the department's SUV was turned into Swiss cheese. The sedan made a tight U-turn and again opened fire at the police officers. This time, several duty officers had exited the station house, firing weapons and attempting to stop the perpetrators from getting away. Several shots had shredded the tires while others had shattered the windows and penetrated the doors. The vehicle veered out of control into a barricade berm and flipped over twice, finally coming to a stop.

Cautiously, several officers approached the wrecked vehicle, weapons at the ready.

'All clear,' one of the officers said. 'No one is coming out of there except in a body bag or being placed on a medical evacuation stretcher.'

The shooting review board was notified of the incident as the bodies were taken to the morgue for autopsies and identification.

'Looks like we won't get out of here until tomorrow at the earliest,' Jack remarked when things had begun to settle down. 'Shooting reviews always seem to take forever to resolve.'

'This time may not be too bad,' Julie added. 'There are plenty of video records and eye witnesses. The interviews will probably take the most time in the investigation process.'

'And here comes our favorite on-the-spot reporter,' said Jamie. 'How's it going, R.R.?'

'Real exciting from where I stood, Doctor,' R.R. answered. 'At a safe distance, with a good view, and out of the line of fire.'

'You're pretty good at protecting your own skin,' Julie scowled, 'aren't you, R.R.?'

'I've had my share of close calls, Detective,' the reporter said, giving Julie the evil eye. 'Six weeks in the hospital then two months in rehab and recovery not that long ago, preceded by nearly being turned into a crispy critter: I'd say that counts as having paid some of my dues.'

'Okay,' Jack acknowledged, 'we'll admit that sometimes you're taking your chances like the rest of us. Through no fault of your own.'

Sam put his hands up in a pleading gesture. 'Let's just admit that when it comes to violent crime, no one is safe.'

R.R. took out a pencil and pad and began writing his report of the shoot-out for his paper.

'Just because I was the only reporter on the scene, doesn't mean that this is an exclusive, Jamie,' he grinned at the group.

209

'I'll need to have exclusive interviews later, too.'

With a two-fingered salute, he walked back to his vehicle and drove back to the offices of the *Midnight Confessor*.

'I can just see the *Confessor's* head-lines, now,' Jack said with disgust. ''Gunfight at the London Corral'. What a mess!'

'Just remember, Jack,' Jamie offered, 'it was his warning that saved our lives.'

★ ★ ★

The next day, after the four detectives had given their statements and been cleared of any misuse of deadly force, the group was finally on their way to Sunnydale. Jack and Julie were informed that a stop would be made at an historic diner near Needles.

'Janey is the third generation owner of the place,' Jamie informed them, 'and she also had a bit part in a scene filmed there when she was just a little girl.'

Jack and Julie asked questions about the diner's history and Janey's experience at the Psychiatric Board and Care. They both shook their heads in astonishment when Sam reported what he and Detective Hector had seen in the bunker building.

'The photos of the woman you sent were shocking enough, but the scene as you've just described it sounds too cruel to be believed,' Julie said almost in disbelief.

'And from what Janey remembers, that's not the worst,' Sam added. 'Many of her memories were repressed until recovered through proper therapeutic methods. Some of them she has never recovered.'

'She must be a strong person to have endured that kind of trauma.' Jack sounded appalled by the report.

The remainder of the trip to Needles was spent in silent contemplation.

★   ★   ★

Anna greeted them as they entered the diner.

'Janey's in the back tallying the receipts from the breakfast rush,' she told them as she led them to an empty table for four. 'She'll want to know that you're back.'

Within moments, Janey came out and was introduced to the two newcomers with Sam and Jamie.

'Pleased to meet you,' she said with a pleasant smile. 'Will you be having lunch today?'

'Iced tea, no lemon, to start,' Julie answered. 'And a side of green salad.'

The others gave similar orders and looked the menus over while the drinks and appetizers were prepared.

After the orders were made and delivered, the lunch crowd and the noon bus started arriving. The noise and bustle allowed the detectives a modicum of privacy as they discussed their strategy. They waited until the rush began to thin and then called Janey over for a quick question and answer session. They attempted to learn everything that they could about the layout of the Sunnydale Psychiatric Board and Care Facility.

'We have come to believe that there is more going on there,' Jamie said, 'than shoddy, unethical therapeutic practices.

Our 'Blue Man' seems to have been involved in felony theft and deadly assault. What's more important is that this man was recently kidnapped and spirited back to Arizona.'

'A man who had been assigned to track this man, down by his company,' Jack continued, 'was attacked twice, possibly by this man. Later, after the man was released from the hospital, he was a fatality in a suspected car bombing. The 'Blue Man' had already been returned to Arizona, so we don't think he was responsible.'

'We have come to believe that Jonah Wilson, AKA 'Blue Man', may be as much a victim as a perpetrator,' Julie added. 'He may be manipulated by drugs and unethical practices that place his mind at the control of vicious and ruthless people.'

'I'm not supposed to talk about what was done to me at that place,' Janey said, 'but that does sound like some of the things that I was put through during my forced three-year stay. One of the examining physicians testified that I had been abused sexually as well as mistreated physically and psychologically. Those were just some of the charges that were brought against the facility. If they've returned to, or continued, those practices, then I hope that you shut them down and put the administration away forever.'

Janey's memory of the buildings was hazy because of the mind and mood altering drugs that were used on her, many of them addictive. She gave the best descriptions that she was able and said that her parents and their lawyers had kept records of the building placements and their stated uses.

When Janey had told them all that she could remember, she went to the back and brought out a stack of old legal documents.

'These were supposed to be under court-ordered seal,' she told them as she placed them on the table, 'But my folks kept copies in case the facility broke their sworn word. I believe that they have proved themselves untrustworthy. Use them as you are able.'

As Sam opened up a briefcase and

placed them inside, he commented, 'These may, or may not, be admissible as evidence, but they could still be invaluable clues. We will see what we can do.'

Having booked two rooms at a nearby motel, the team left the diner, prepared to go over all that they had learned and decide how to use their latest knowledge. The discussion and planning session lasted until nearly midnight when Jamie and Julie decided to call it a night. Sam and Jack stayed up for another hour before agreeing that they had done all that they could with their current data.

'I want another look at that building at the edge of the facility,' Sam said as he readied for bed. 'There was too much that Detective Hector and I didn't have time to check out. That woman was almost comatose and looked malnourished to me.'

'And I don't like the fact that they are at least using that woman for diabolical experiments,' Jack stated angrily. 'No one has the right to abuse another human being for their own gain.'

'We still don't know exactly what they

are doing in that building,' Sam replied. 'But it is certain that the woman was being mistreated.'

17

Joseph Johnstein took Rachael's body into one of the locked rooms, intending to take her back to her office where her body would be found and the autopsy would show that she had died of cardiac arrest.

'Not even Kindle and Roarschack know everything that I'm doing here,' he said as he gently laid the body on the bed. 'You were an interesting diversion, my dear, but your curiosity was your downfall.'

Relocking the door, Johnstein returned to room 4B.

★   ★   ★

When everyone was asleep and the grounds were quiet, a male figure carrying a heavy load on his shoulders approached the private offices of the administrators and staff. Careful not to make noise, he fumbled for the key to a particular door. After unlocking the door, he looked for a place to lay his load down. Finding the place he wanted, he undid the sack and removed a body. Then he arranged it so that it looked as if it fallen from the office chair.

'Goodbye, sweet Rachael,' he whispered as he exited, locking the door after himself.

In the morning, when Rachael Bennet did not show for the scheduled morning meeting, two orderlies were sent to find her. They checked her office and found the door locked. When they could not get a response, they obtained a key. Inside, they found Rachael lying on the floor behind her desk. An ambulance was called to the scene. The Sunnydale police arrived seconds later and quickly cordoned off the office.

'Who was she?' the officers asked when the ambulance doctor had pronounced her as deceased.

'Medical therapist Rachael Bennet,' Dr. Roarschack responded, a stricken look on his face. 'She was too young to just die like that.'

'Did she have any medical problems?' the doctor asked. 'She may have had a stroke or a heart attack. Or she may have had some other complication.'

'None of us knew of anything,' Dr. Kindle replied. 'She always seemed to be in good health.'

The shocked crowd watched as the body was loaded into the ambulance and driven to the hospital's morgue.

'I want a complete forensic workup of the office and the body,' the lead detective told his team. 'Detectives from out of state have been asking a lot of questions recently. I want to be sure that this was not an unnatural death.'

★   ★   ★

The four detectives arrived at the Sunnydale police headquarters just as the investigative team was returning.

'Detective Ronson?' Sam asked when he saw them in the parking lot.

A tall man of about forty turned and looked at him. 'Yes? Can I help you?'

Sam introduced himself and the others

with him. 'We have papers requesting search warrants at the Sunnydale Psychiatric Board and Care Facility.'

'We just came from there, Lieutenant,' Ronson replied after being introduced and viewing the group's credentials. 'A young woman was found dead in her office this morning. Preliminary forensic evidence indicates death by natural causes. An autopsy is also being conducted to be certain.'

'May I attend the exam?' Jamie asked. 'I'm a credentialed FME with the LPD.'

'I have to be there myself, Dr. Watson,' Detective Ronson said. 'I'll vouch for your being there. It is to be done in a couple of hours.'

'Thank you, Detective.'

'Is there somewhere we could confer in private, Detective?' Sam requested. 'There are some things that we need to discuss before the formal request is made for the search and seizure warrants.'

'I'll locate a conference room,' Ronson replied.

After their meeting, Detective Ronson's partner took Sam to the judge that handled the legal processes for the warrants while

Jamie and Ronson viewed the autopsy.

'The deceased seems to have had a cardiac arrest,' the ME explained. 'We'll be looking for evidence of heart disease, stroke, and/or any other signs of an unknown debilitating condition.'

'Will you be conducting blood and tissue samples?' Jamie asked. 'There are many drugs that can simulate death from natural causes. The operators of the facility are under suspicion of acting unethically as well as illegally. As such, one of them may be trying to cover-up his wrongdoing.'

'These things are good to know, Dr. Watson,' she was answered. 'The facility has had a past, though unsubstantiated, history of problems.'

★　★　★

After the judge heard Sam's reasonable causes and had seen the evidence, he issued the search warrants that were asked for. Detective Sheldon went with him, Julie, and Jack to the facility grounds.

'There is a building just at the edge of the property that I wish to see as well as the hospital rooms and the board and care rooms,' Sam explained. 'Several men were observed taking a man-sized bundle into it after we were informed of the kidnapping of one of our persons of interest.'

'The warrant allows us to check all offices, residences, and buildings on the property,' Sheldon said. 'I think we can show cause to enter that building as well.'

Sam and Sheldon gathered several uniformed officers and headed to their destination.

★   ★   ★

While the search warrants were being executed, the autopsy proceeded in the usual manner. Jamie watched closely as each procedure was recorded.

'The heart and lungs all seem healthy,' the ME explained. 'Sometimes, though, there is no previous indication of a problem. I'll check for signs of coronary blockages now. Maybe we'll find an undetected blood clot or other cause of sudden failure.'

'How long before the toxicology tests are complete?' Detective Ronson wanted to know.

'Fortunately,' the ME answered, 'the lab has no backlog at this time. We should get an answer within forty-eight to seventy-two hours.'

'Lt. Holmes and Detective Ronson will have completed their search before then,' Jamie said. 'Perhaps they will find something for a 'cease and desist' type of order.'

Jamie waited while the heart valves, chambers and vessels were checked. When there was no evidence of catastrophic failure, Jamie joined her colleagues.

'The body showed no probable evidence against a sudden and catastrophic cardiac arrest and there were no indications of any other contributing factors,' Jamie informed Detectives Ronson and Roberts. 'The heart muscle showed no indicating factors of heart disease, nor the brain of a stroke. The ME has ordered a work up of the blood and tissue samples in an effort to make a definite determination for the woman's death. My gut feeling is that she was given an injection of some kind that caused her heart to stop.'

'Dr. Watson.' The ME came out of the autopsy room looking unsettled. 'When I was closing up the body, I noticed a small puncture wound in her neck, right at the hairline.'

'As someone might do if they wanted to hide the fact that she had been injected with something, Dr. MacMillen?' Jamie inquired.

'The stereo zoom also showed something interesting,' Dr. MacMillen added. 'Come back and I'll show you.'

Back in the autopsy room, Jamie found the body on its side, the hair at the nape of the neck pulled out of the way of an area with a small red bump. Jamie, having replaced her surgical scrubs and gloves, began palpating and examining the area.

'This was definitely made by a hypodermic needle,' she gave her opinion. 'It, or the substance that was injected, appears to have irritated the site. Can we get a photograph?'

'That has already been done,' Dr.

MacMillen replied. 'Now, take a look through the stereo zoom and give me your opinion please, Doctor.'

Under the powerful magnification, Jamie saw what appeared to be a hair with the follicle still attached.

'This is not the same type of hair as the deceased's,' Jamie observed. 'Hand me the forceps, please.'

Jamie carefully plucked the hair from the puncture wound and had it placed in a labeled evidence container that detailed the chain of evidence.

'We'll run this through the DNA database to see if there's a match,' Dr. MacMillen said as she placed the bag with the rest of the collected evidence. 'How do you suppose it got there?'

'Perhaps we'll never know,' Jamie replied. 'Just chalk it up to our good fortune that it's there and the follicle is still attached.'

★   ★   ★

At the psychiatric facility's gate, Detective Sheldon showed the gate attendant the search and seizure warrants.

'These warrants authorize the city of Sunnydale and the state of Arizona access to search all buildings and offices and to interview such individuals as deemed necessary,' he ordered. 'Do *not* touch that phone or any buttons or switches inside the gatehouse, nor any of your communication devices. The facility personnel are to have no advance warning.'

'Several of these officers will stay behind to assure your compliance,' Julie added. 'Are we clear on that?'

The attendant nodded, and then showed one of the Sunnydale police officers how to open the gate. Detective Sheldon, Lt. Holmes, and Sgt. Simon, along with two other officers, headed for the windowless building as the rest headed toward their assigned offices, residential areas, and recreational centers.

'The apparently unguarded door is over here,' Sam pointed out to his group. 'The room that we are looking for is 4B.'

The law enforcers from Arizona and California approached with extreme caution. The door on the south side of the building again opened to the inside with a gentle push.

'When we were here the last time,' Sam said softly, 'the door did not seem to be alarmed. However, our adversaries may have had time to change that, so be extremely cautious.'

Once inside, Sam proceeded down the hallway to the door where he had last seen the woman in his cell phone photos.

'The woman who was here may have been moved.' He gently tried the door. It gave easily, but the room had no appearance of recent occupancy.

'The dead woman may have found out what was going on and been silenced,' Sheldon opined. 'The body could have been staged to appear as a sudden, but natural, death.'

'If our theories are correct,' Julie said, 'that would be a viable scenario. She did seem to be young and healthy.'

'I think that she saw someone using the woman in an illegal, and possibly obscene, manner,' Sam added. 'The scene that I saw definitely indicated physical, and possibly, sexual abuse. The sooner we find out what has been going on, the sooner we can shut this place down and get some real help for these people.'

★ ★ ★

The teams quickly secured all of the designated buildings, rooms, and offices. Near total surprise was achieved and none of the people who were on the list for questioning got away. Of course the person that should have been on the list wasn't even suspected or known as someone who was involved.

Joseph Johnstein had slipped the net and was gone from the grounds by the time everything was effectively locked down. Fuming as he drove the backroads to his home, he tried several times to contact his team of hitmen. He became increasingly frustrated and angry on the drive home.

'Something has gone wrong in California,' he told himself. 'Goliath should have reported in by now, and this raid should never have been made. I must pack and leave a message that says that I have had to leave on sudden and important business out of the country.'

Using his computer and a secure credit card, he booked a circuitous flight to a small country that had no extradition treaty with the US. Everything was so spontaneous that he was sure that he would be able to leave without being stopped at any of the airports along his escape route.

'Sometimes, too much planning can be worse having no plan at all,' he said to himself as he pulled into his driveway.

★　★　★

Jamie and Jack had checked on Rachael Bennet's known associates and turned up a man who had connections to both Rachael and to the facility. When they found out that he was the youngest son of one of the original founders who had retired during the Atfield debacle of thirty years ago and had been seen often in Rachael's company, they decided to ask the Arizona authorities to place an APB out for him at all routes of exit from the state or country.

'He's got to be involved somehow,' Julie said. 'His relationship to the Sunnydale facility has got to be more than just a coincidence.'

'The connection has got to be there,' Jack agreed. 'Let's hope that we can catch him before he gets away.'

The APB and BOLO requests went out as quickly as the computer could make them. Within minutes, a report came back that a Joseph Abram Johnstein had booked passage on several flights from the US to Europe, Africa, and Pakistan.

'A flight just left for Heathrow airport five minutes ago,' Julie said. 'Johnstein's itinerary has him on a connecting flight for Egypt half an hour after he arrives in England. Let's see if we can have him stopped at the US airport or in England and returned to Arizona.'

'I'll see if we can get a standby flight to France, with an open ticket to his Egyptian airport while you make the arrangements,' Jack said. 'If the British authorities miss him, maybe we'll catch up to him there.'

'Good. I'll leave Sam and Julie a text

telling them what we've found out and what we are planning.'

★   ★   ★

As Johnstein boarded his connecting flight to England, several sky marshals approached the boarding line and began checking IDs, passports, and boarding passes.

'We're looking for a man wanted for questioning regarding a situation in Arizona,' the marshal in charge told the boarding attendant. 'He would be in his late 50s or early 60s and possibly well-dressed.'

'Several men have already boarded who could have matched that description,' the attendant said, 'but their passports and boarding passes showed them to all to be British citizens returning home from holiday.'

A commotion in the line caught the attention of the attendant and the marshal.

'But I tell you, sir,' a well-dressed man with an Oxford accent said indignantly as he was pulled out of line, 'this is not my passport! Someone must have stolen mine and switched it out!'

The marshal, who was checking the man's papers, said, 'If you'll just step over here, we'll clear this up as quickly as we can; and we'll see that *if* your story checks out and you've missed your flight, that you *will* get home.'

'I shall lodge a complaint with her Majesty's government, sir!' the belligerent man replied, 'I thought that our nations were friends!'

The man was gently, but firmly, led off to a private room for further interrogation.

No one else attracted the attention of the sky marshals and the plane was allowed to move to the take-off line.

* * *

When the big jumbo jet taxied into the take-off position, Johnstein felt relieved. He relaxed in his seat as the plane sped down the jet-way. In seconds, the plane lifted off the tarmac and the wheels thumped into their flight position. The first hurdle had been jumped. Barring an unforeseen emergency, the plane would not stop until it landed in London, England at its scheduled time. Now was the time to take a well-deserved nap.

18

Sam, Julie and Detective Sheldon divided their forces into teams and thoroughly searched the building. In several rooms, paraphernalia and pharmaceuticals of an unknown usage were found and tagged as evidence.

'We'll need Dr. Watson and your ME to see all of this in situ,' Sam observed. 'One, or both, may possibly have an educated guess about all of this.'

'I agree,' Sheldon said. 'Dr. MacMillen has often helped to solve a case with her ability to think outside the box.'

'Then she and Dr. Watson should be a formidable team,' observed Julie.

As they continued to search the building, three rooms were found to have been recently occupied and hurriedly abandoned.'

'These devices,' one of the officers said, looking pale and weak, 'were used for torture, not for therapy! No one should have *ever* been subjected to their use. These are inhumane and inhuman.'

A surreptitious movement caught the eye of one of the other officers.

'Freeze!' she shouted. 'Now, put your hands on the top of your head and walk backwards, slowly, toward the sound of my voice!'

'Don't hurt me!' a frightened voice sobbed. 'Please don't hurt me anymore!'

Slowly, a naked and disheveled female backed away from a dark corner, hands on her head, as she had been ordered.

'Someone get a blanket for her,' Julie said in a choked voice. 'We need to get her to a hospital as soon as possible. She's been beaten and God knows what else.'

'Those look like scars from restraints and bruises from fists or blunt instruments,' Sam added. 'She's going to need lots of physical and psychiatric therapy to work through the trauma she's been put through. Treat her gently, people. She needs TLC more than we need the answers that she can give.'

'We have a therapist on call specializing in just this kind of need,' Sheldon told them, dialing his cell phone. 'We have found one wounded little bird, there may be others. Let's see if we can find and rescue them.'

★   ★   ★

When the search of the windowless building had been made, three more people were found; two young women and a teenage boy, all in various stages of trauma and physical condition. In a room off by itself, the bodies of Jonah Wilson and a woman of indeterminate age were found lying strapped to hospital beds. The looks of terror and horror on their dead faces were the stuff that night terrors were made of.

'These people were obviously tortured to death,' a pale and shaken officer from the Arizona Highway Patrol remarked. 'I've never seen such acts of cruelty. And by people who have supposedly taken an oath to 'first, do no harm'.'

Arrangements to transfer the patients of the Sunnydale Board and Care Facility were made and, after a quick evaluation of each person's physical and mental state, implemented. The two bodies were taken to the city morgue for autopsies to be scheduled.

'When the treatment records are reviewed,' Sheldon wondered, 'how many more deaths will we find? Thirty years of cover-up and this is just now coming to light! And to think that we were all so unaware of what was going on here.'

'Evil is like mushrooms,' Julie said. 'It grows best in darkness.'

★   ★   ★

Back in Needles at Janey's 'Nostalgia Diner', the detective team sat at a table, bringing Janey Atfield, her crew and Detectives Hector and Roberts to date on the happenings in Sunnydale.

'The place has been closed and all of the doctors, orderlies, and other staff are being questioned,' Sam told them. 'All of the records have been seized and are being reviewed by a licensing board of inquiry before non-confidential inter-views and the like are turned over to the state's Criminal Justice districts for prosecution.'

'You won't have to worry about violating the court's gag order, either, Janey,' Jamie informed her. 'A judge has ordered the records of your settlement opened and reviewed for possible illegalities.'

'The only drawback now,' Julie added, 'is that a probable major player may have gotten away.'

'Who is that?' Detective Hector asked, a frown marring his facial expression. 'Will he send more men to the diner to intimidate Ms. Atfield?'

'I don't believe so,' Jack replied. 'At least I don't see him having the time or resources with all of the airports along his scheduled itinerary on alert and Interpol looking for him. He slipped out of the country when he stole and exchanged passports with a British national with whom he had an uncanny resemblance.

'The people at the London airport leg of schedule will be checking all entry and returning passports. The British embassy has issued its citizen a new, and specially flagged, passport so that he can return home.'

Johnstein had come prepared with a second, and false, passport. When he saw the intense security at the customs counter for incoming flights, he was glad that he had. At his first opportunity, he got rid of his stolen passport.

The British officials scrutinized the exiting passengers and checked their passports. They were hampered by not having a recent photo or an adequate description of the man they wanted. Johnstein walked right through customs without getting a second look or having to answer more than routine questions. Johnstein also had used some cotton wadding between his cheeks and gums. Anyone who looked at him would not know why they were sure that this was not the person they were looking for, but would not question their observation.

As he walked up to the customs counter, his false passport was given a cursory look and he was told to proceed on to the baggage claim area. His claim check would normally have given him a moment of uneasiness, but he had hurdled so many obstacles at this point that he felt safe in the assumption that he was home free at this leg of his journey. Having picked up his two suitcases, he continued on to the waiting area for the next leg of his journey.

★　★　★

Sam and Jamie were preparing to board their flight to Paris, France.

'How did you get permission for this flight?' Jamie asked. 'Has the travel budget been increased to let us do this?'

'No,' Sam declared. 'I just volunteered us take a leave-without-pay and bought the tickets from my own pocket. The commissioner and the mayor were just too happy to let us do this on our own. If we screw this up, we take the fall and the city has plausible deniability.'

'So that's why it's just you and me?'

'Yep.'

'Not that I'm complaining, but if this blows up in our faces, does that mean that I crash and burn with you?'

'You can back out anytime you want. No hard feelings.'

'And break up a record setting team? 'All for one and one for all'.'

The cab to the airport arrived and they stayed silent all the way.

As the cab pulled up to the curb, Sam told Jamie, 'Great-grandpa's fraternal grandmother was related to a famous French artist. I have been to a distant cousin's home in France before, and I've made arrangements for us to stay at his summer home while we're in Paris.'

'It must be nice to have connections,' Jamie said.

★　★　★

The flight to France was not as smooth as it could have been. They were flying into a headwind with a lot of turbulence for about half of the trip. The captain apologized again and again as he attempted to get above or around the rough weather.

'There is a major storm over the Atlantic and the air is exceedingly rough. However, we are currently in no danger, and we should eventually pass out of the storm,' he told his passengers. 'This storm was one of those that can't be predicted very far in advance. That's how we got caught up in it.'

'This must be especially frightening for first-time flyers,' Sam commented to Jamie, who sat white-knuckled in her seat next to him.

'And to those of us that have never had to fly through a storm before!' Jamie replied. 'All of the sudden ups and downs are very scary. It's enough to make even a seasoned flyer think twice about air travel!'

Once the plane had passed the bad weather, the flight was smooth and the landing was routine and without incident.

Sam's distant cousin, Jean-Paul, was waiting at the customs passenger unloading area after they had gotten their luggage.

'I heard about that god-awful storm,' Jean-Paul greeted them after they exited from customs. 'I believe that was what you would call a 'hundred-year storm'. I'm happy to see that the plane and all aboard made the crossing safely.'

'I think that trip has probably just shortened my life span by a few years,' Jamie half-joked after Sam had made introductions all around. 'I hope that the return trip will be less eventful.'

'*Mais oui, Mademoiselle* Watson,' the Frenchman smiled at her.

Jean-Paul helped Sam and Jamie put their suitcases in the trunk of his vehicle and then got behind the wheel to take them to his summer home in the city.

For American tourists, the drive was one to remind them of certain amusement rides. Both of the Frenchman's passengers were relieved when the small car pulled into the driveway of a modest villa.

The car was unloaded and everything was taken inside. Jean-Paul gave instructions to the waiting servants as to which rooms his guests were staying and to place their things there.

'I hope that eight o'clock is not too late for your evening meal,' he said to them.

'That must be somewhere around lunchtime in California,' Sam said, calculating the time difference.

'Ah, I had not taken that into account,' his cousin frowned. 'Perhaps you would prefer something a little lighter?'

'No, that will be alright,' Jamie said graciously. 'The sooner we get acclimated to the time changes, the sooner we'll overcome the jet lag; or at least that is what I've been told.'

'But have you not crossed the ocean before, Dr. Watson?'

'That was more than a year ago, and with a lot things that kept us occupied, Jean-Paul.'

'As the international news reported,' Jean-Paul replied. 'A very dangerous affair, no?'

★ ★ ★

Sam and Jamie allowed Jean-Paul to show them the sights as they waited for news of their quarry. Jean-Paul was proud of his home city's history and many tourist stops.

'The Eiffel Tower was once known as the tallest structure in the world and many lovers' meet for their trysts,' their guide pointed out triumphantly. 'Even the German armies of both world wars would not desecrate it.'

'I wonder if, with all of the recent changes in moral and cultural attitudes, if an invading army or terrorist group would feel the same way today,' remarked Sam thoughtfully.

'Many of the younger set would be beside themselves with glee to see the artifacts from the bourgeoisie past fall into permanent ruin,' answered Jean-Paul with a sad sigh.

★ ★ ★

When they returned to Jean-Paul's summer home, they found that a messenger had just arrived.

'Telegram for M. Holmes,' she said, holding out a sealed envelope as she added, 'I've been asked to await a reply.'

Sam tore open the envelope and read the contents. As he handed the envelope to Jamie, he took a pencil and a note pad and wrote, 'Will proceed to next stop via midnight train. Forward next, care of nearest hotel.' That will be all, thank you,' he told the messenger as he paid the message fee and added a generous tip.

'It would seem,' Jamie sighed regretfully, 'that we won't get to see any more of your historic city, Jean-Paul.'

'There will be no rest for these weary travelers,' Sam added. 'Maybe we'll have more time for sightseeing the next time we visit Paris.'

Preparations were made for the next leg of their trip and then Sam and Jamie both laid down for a short rest before the evening meal.

After supper, Sam and Jamie made sure that everything would be ready when the car came to take them to the train station.

The train was on time and their trip to a station near the Suez Canal was uneventful.

'It would seem that Johnstein has prepared for something like this for some time,' Jamie observed. 'The false papers, the multipart travel plans, and the disguises are not something made up in the spur of the moment.'

'I agree,' Sam nodded. 'Our adversary has carefully planned his moves in case of such a setback in advance.'

'When, and where,' Jamie wished to know, 'will we catch up with Johnstein?'

'Hopefully,' Sam advised her, 'before he reaches one of the fanatical anti-western groups. Many of them would willingly hide a fugitive from our laws, if only to further their own agendas.'

19

Joseph Johnstein had changed his looks and travel plans several times since leaving Sunnydale, Arizona, USA. Each time, he had barely eluded the people who had been set upon his trail. He was beginning to grow weary with all of the last minute changes in his plans. After this next stop, he felt that he would at last lose his pursuers and vanish into protective camouflage.

★　★　★

When the truck bearing foodstuffs pulled up to the train platform, Sam watched the man pretending to be of near-eastern origins get out and go to the ticket office.

'Jamie,' he whispered. 'Our 'Person of Interest' has arrived. We have just moments to affect his capture.'

Quickly, Sam and Jamie approached the tired looking man.

'Joseph Johnstein,' Sam called to him. 'You are wanted for questioning back in the US in relation to various and sundry proceedings at the Sunnydale Psychiatric Board and Care Facility and for what you know of the actions of one Jonah Wilson while he was in California after apparently having escaped from the facility's care.'

Johnstein started to run, but Jamie had stepped into his path.

'I'm sorry, Mr. Johnstein,' she said with menace in her demeanor, 'but you *will* be coming with us, whether you wish to or not. You can come along quietly, or trussed up like a Christmas turkey. It's your choice.'

Johnstein charged at Jamie, thinking that she would be the easier to escape from. Jamie side-stepped him, and with quick moves had him on the ground where Sam quickly cuffed his hands behind his back.

'Not all women,' Sam said as he jerked the man to his feet, 'are easily intimidated or overpowered. Some, like the good Dr. Watson, do not take kindly to caveman tactics and know how to counter them.

You are now charged with assault upon a police officer. When we return to the States, we will see what other charges await you.'

Sam, using a British police whistle, signaled for back-up and a vehicle to transport their prisoner to a local holding facility while the extradition papers were filed.

In twenty-four hours, a US Marshal arrived to take custody for the transportation back to Arizona. Sam and Jamie recognized the marshal when he walked into their hotel to join them in finalizing the paperwork.

'Marshal Fox?' Sam asked.

'Detective Holmes.' Marshall Newton Fox held out his hand. 'It's good to see you and Dr. Watson looking so well after your adventures in England. I hear that you've recently been promoted?'

'Yes, and they put me in charge of a team back in California,' Sam replied. 'Of course, Holmes has to have his Dr. Watson, so she's on the team, too.'

'Well, let's go get the prisoner processed for extradition, shall we?'

After due process, Johnstein and his

guards arrived back in Arizona and the charges read. The prisoner was Mirandized and given a chance to obtain a lawyer.

* * *

The church was filled with flowers and well-wishers. The bride was ravishing in her pale pink wedding gown. The groom's face was filled with love as his bride walked down the aisle. The parents of the bride both had tears in their eyes as their daughter and her husband-to-be exchanged their vows.

After the ceremony was completed, the guests retired to the reception room.

'I'm so happy for you, Bobbie.' Julie wept tears of joy. 'I wish sometimes that Jonathan and I hadn't drifted apart while he was at the university back East.'

Sam, watching the happy couple in their first dance, looked at Jamie and thought, 'Good friends often make good life partners. Do I dare to hope?'

Jamie suddenly caught Sam's eye. 'He's a good man and he treats me with respect. Could we take things to the next step?'

We do hope that you have enjoyed reading this large print book.

Did you know that all of our titles are available for purchase?

We publish a wide range of high quality large print books including:
Romances, Mysteries, Classics
General Fiction
Non Fiction and Westerns

Special interest titles available in large print are:
The Little Oxford Dictionary
Music Book, Song Book
Hymn Book, Service Book

Also available from us courtesy of Oxford University Press:
Young Readers' Dictionary
(large print edition)
Young Readers' Thesaurus
(large print edition)

For further information or a free brochure, please contact us at:
Ulverscroft Large Print Books Ltd.,
The Green, Bradgate Road, Anstey,
Leicester, LE7 7FU, England.
Tel: (00 44) **0116 236 4325**
Fax: (00 44) **0116 234 0205**

VILLAGE OF FEAR

Noel Lee

After narrowly escaping death on a train, two people find themselves in an eerie deserted village — and make a grisly discovery . . . On a dark and stormy night, locals gather in an inn to tell a frightening tale . . . A writer's country holiday gets off to a bad start when he finds a corpse in his cottage . . . And a death under the dryer at a fashionable hairdressing salon leads to several beneficiaries of the late lady's will falling under suspicion of murder . . .

PUNITIVE ACTION

John Robb

Soldiers of Fort Valeau, a Foreign Legion outpost, discover the mutilated bodies of several men from their overdue relief column, ambushed and massacred by Dylaks. Captain Monclaire's radio report to the garrison at Dini Sadazi results in a promise that more soldiers will be despatched to Valeau, from there to mount punitive action against the offenders. But before the reinforcements arrive, the Dylaks send a message to Monclaire — if he does not surrender, they will attack and conquer the fort . . .

DEATH WALKS SKID ROW

Michael Mallory

Sunset Boulevard, 1975: Two men are speeding home from a party on a night that will haunt them forever. Despite the dangerously wet roads, both passenger and driver are very drunk. Thirty years later on Los Angeles's Skid Row, a homeless man is found dead in an alley. Discovering several disturbing connections, reporter Ramona Rios and a man known on Skid Row only as 'the governor' set out on separate paths to unveil the truth, but are brought together to face a perilous web of power, manipulation and deceit.

ONCE YOU STOP, YOU'RE DEAD

Eaton K. Goldthwaite

The USS *Slocum* is on a routine naval patrol northwest of Bermuda when the SOS crackles over the radio. Cuban National Air's Flight Twelve is ditching in the Atlantic with eighty-nine passengers and five crew aboard. Commander H.P. Perry readies his ship for standard rescue operations — only to discover there's nothing standard about the survivors. Once aboard, they're more demanding than grateful, for most are Russian or Cuban nationals. That's when Commander Perry realizes he's an unwitting pawn in a deadly game, the outcome of which could have grave international repercussions . . .

MURDER GETS AROUND

Robert Sidney Bowen

Murder and mayhem begin innocently enough at the Rankins' cocktail party, where Gerry Barnes and his fiery red-haired girlfriend Paula Grant while away a few carefree hours. There, Gerry meets René DeFoe, who wishes to engage his services as a private investigator, for undisclosed reasons — an assignment Gerry reluctantly accepts. But the next morning, when Gerry enters his office to keep his appointment, he finds René murdered on the premises. He puts his own life at risk as he investigates why a corpse was made of his client . . .

THE FREE TRADERS

Victor Rousseau

The Free Traders deal fur and whisky, debouching their way through the Canadian northern territories. Pitted against them are the country's soldier-police, the Northwest Mounted. Lee Anderson, Royal Canadian Mounted Police sergeant, is on a mission to find a man wanted for murder twenty-five years ago. But when he and a mysterious woman are thrown down a cliff by a dynamite explosion, her memory disappears from the shock, and they find themselves in a wilderness pursued by the Free Traders — who are bent on killing Lee and capturing the woman.